THE WIND WAGON

Sheriff Al Corning was as tough as they came and with his four seasoned deputies he kept the peace in Laramie — at least until the squatters came. To fend off starvation, the settlers took some cattle off the cowmen, including Jonas Lefler. A hard, unforgiving man, Lefler retaliated with lynchings. Things got worse when one of the squatters revealed he was a former Texas lawman — and no mean shooter. Could Sheriff Corning prevent further bloodshed?

TROY HOWARD

THE WIND WAGON

Complete and Unabridged

LINFORD
Leicester

First published in Great Britain in 1997 by
Robert Hale Limited
London

First Linford Edition
published 1999
by arrangement with
Robert Hale Limited
London

British Library CIP Data

Howard, Troy, *1916 –*
    The wind wagon.—Large print ed.—
Linford western library
    1. Western stories
    2. Large type books
    I. Title
    813.5′4 [F]

ISBN 0–7089–5473–1   531388 a

Published by
F. A. Thorpe (Publishing) Ltd.
Anstey, Leicestershire

Set by Words & Graphics Ltd.
Anstey, Leicestershire
Printed and bound in Great Britain by
T. J. International Ltd., Padstow, Cornwall

This book is printed on acid-free paper

1

Face to Face

The Laramie Plains were to a great extent without trees. The winters were brutal with week-long snow storms, weather so bitterly cold that regardless of long johns, heavy woollen shirts and sheep-pelt-lined horsehide coats, the chill penetrated.

Each springtime revealed cattle, horses, and people, frozen to death.

Springtime was less cold. It had to be or nothing which derived its life support from the earth would either appear or survive.

The summers in the high plains country had cold nights, pleasant days, even hot days. A bountiful range country could not be bountiful otherwise.

But there was one force of nature

1

that, winter or summer, it was almost impossible to escape from. Wind.

Wintertime it screamed and howled; summertime its force compelled people to bend into it. The people who lived in that kind of country were right about one thing: they said it was necessary to have harsh, wet winters in order to have warm, fecund summers. Few contested that, but what was the reason for wind?

The soldier compound over at Fort Laramie was an eerie place when the wind blew. It had been abandoned after the last Indian campaign had been concluded.

Its dilapidated condition was not entirely due to the lack of garrisoned men to maintain it. There were a number of Laramie's residents who made the short trip to the old fort with wagons which they loaded with hardware, doors, window-casings, firewood logs from the old palisades, and other things such as hinges, knobs, even candle holders which could not be readily acquired in the town of Laramie or, if they could be acquired, cost more than inhabitants had to spend.

Subsequent to the passing of Red Cloud and his fighting clans cattlemen came. They had come earlier but although Indians did not care for beef they were not above stampeding herds, using cow hides for tipis formerly covered with buffalo hides.

The bison were also gone. The early cattlemen who had hung on, and whose hatred of Indians was deep, were a tough, resourceful and indomitable breed.

With millions of acres of grassland, no fences, no boundaries and no Indians, they prospered. Laramie in fact became a cow town, meaning a large proportion of its livelihood derived from cattle.

Where the railroad tracks passed close, the stockmen had created a series of corrals with loading chutes.

Newcomers to the Laramie Plains country could be as dense as oak and still understand that cattle interests dominated not just the livelihoods of local people but also ruled millions of acres of free-graze country.

It was a feudal territory. The established ranchers owned local banks, blocks of business buildings; what political life existed did so only with the approval of cow interests.

With the vanquishment of the Indians, the arrival of railroad tracks, the telegraph, a good network of roads like veins leading in all directions, Laramie had to prosper and it did.

There were four churches, the only white-painted one, the Southern Baptist, had the largest congregation.

There were three smithies, two mercantile establishments, a genuine hotel, several rooming-houses and a physician named Loomis who not only doctored but extracted teeth.

There were several saloons but the Palace was the most popular, largest and most elegant. It had gaslight chandeliers which made small hissing sounds which were drowned out by customers, rangemen, their employers, merchants and a boldly lettered sign which said No Ladies Allowed.

The jailhouse was a reminder of times before a planing mill came to Laramie. After that innovation, buildings had planed wooden sidings. The jailhouse was made of logs, had adzed marks and other scars.

It had an office where the Sheriff of Albany County, Alfred Corning, worked, an offshoot of the original structure which had six prisoners' cells, three on each side of a narrow hallway.

The sheriff had four deputies as lawlessness had been a way of life since the first hide hunters settled-in. Al Corning was a large-boned, weathered man, in many ways as hard as iron, in other ways a tolerant individual.

He'd had his hands full since accepting the sheriff's job five years earlier. His deputies were seasoned lawmen, hard riders and uncompromising individuals who took their oath to uphold the law very seriously.

The lawman before Al Corning had been killed by ambushing renegade Indians. He too had been well liked. When the deputized posse riders concluded their manhunt they left behind six renegades hanging from the same tree.

Sheriff Corning's law-enforcement activities had been more or less routine until the railroad company, which had been granted every other mile along its route, began posting notices in cities and towns east of the Missouri River, offering land for fifty cents an acre.

Initially the flow of outlanders was a trickle. Because many came without funds, Al Corning and his deputies rode themselves ragged catching cattle thieves, a variety of people cattle interests despised above all others and who, when rangemen caught them, were hanged out of hand without the sheriff's knowledge until weeping widows and mothers came to town in hysterics.

Al Corning was called before the town council not once but twice to explain how these murders happened and what he had been doing to catch the hangmen.

The sheriff told his favourite deputy, Rufus Kelly, he intended to ride down the hangmen if it required being in the saddle every day for a month, and Rufe Kelly dryly said, 'It wouldn't take near that long. You know as well as I do who's doing this. The last two times I dug up the hides where the starving sod busters buried 'em. The same brand was on both hides — Circle L.'

Corning shifted in his desk chair and cleared his throat. Kelly said, 'Al, you can't blame 'em. The railroad sold 'em land. They came out here to settle on an' farm, and starve out. They don't belong here. It's not farmin' country. They got families. They can't watch 'em starve.'

The sheriff leaned on his desk looking

at his large, scarred hands. 'It's got to stop,' he said, and raised his eyes.

Rufe Kelly made a death's-head grin. 'We'd need an army. Them cowmen are thicker'n thieves. If we go out yonder and arrest old Jonas Lefler's Circle L riders the gawdamned sky's going to fall on us. We'll have a range war.'

The sheriff leaned back off his desk looking steadily at his chief deputy. He knew, possibly better than the burly man across from him, that cattle interests ruled his county and beyond.

Rufe Kelly anticipated what could have been in the lawman's mind, 'Talk won't do it, Al. Maybe with the squatters it might. By now they're scairt enough to listen. But there's not a rancher out there who'd listen. They are their own law an' you know it.'

'Rufe, it's the law!'

Kelly threw up his hands and would have left his chair if the sheriff hadn't said more. 'There's soldiers over at

Cheyenne, that's no more'n twenty-five, thirty miles from here.'

Kelly sat in silence for a long moment before speaking. 'Do you know what you're saying? Not just a range war but the cowmen've got lots of influence at the capitol.'

Corning looked steadily at his deputy. 'If we look the other way those damned squatters'll get to relying on rustled beef and the cowmen'll do like they did elsewhere, they'll declare their own war, an' we'll be in the middle with both sides hatin' our guts.'

Corning shot forward, clasped both hands together on the desk and said, 'All right, *you* tell *me* what the answer is?'

Rufe Kelly shook his head. 'I don't know. All's I do know is that the lynching's got to stop.'

'Agreed. And how about the thievin' bastards that get hung?'

Kelly relaxed in his chair, let his gaze wander to the gun rack on the west wall with its chain running through trigger guards with a large padlock at the end.

Sheriff Corning said, 'I'm waiting, Rufe.'

Kelly's hard, blue gaze returned to the lawman's face as he said, 'I don't know.'

Corning made a humourless small smile. 'Neither do I, but the lynching's got to stop. Are you sure them was Circle L marks on the hides you dug up?'

Kelly nodded without speaking, and the sheriff leaned off his desk as though to arise as he spoke again. 'Let's go talk to Mister Lefler.'

Kelly shoved up out of the chair, watched the sheriff unlock the binder at the gun rack, pull it loose, let the chain fall and took down two Winchester saddle guns. He tossed one to his deputy, pointed to a saddle boot for the carbine and said, 'You know anything about this reincarnation talk?' and when his deputy stared the sheriff said the rest of it. 'I must've been a real son of a bitch in some other life. Let's go.'

They got their animals from the liveryman's corral, led them inside to be rigged out and the liveryman, a tall, rangy individual who only shaved every other week, leaned on a three-tined feed fork watching and saying nothing.

The wind was blowing, which was not unusual even in summertime. Not hard but just hard enough to make conversation difficult.

Once Rufe Kelly said, 'I wish to hell it'd been the brand of someone else.'

Corning nodded without answering back.

Jonas Lefler was one of those old-timers who had fought and scrabbled and shot his way to the top. No one knew how old he was nor did it matter. He didn't carry an ounce of spare meat, wore a perpetual squint — something which went with living in windy country — and was the unofficial spokesman for the ranchers in all directions, even

11

over as far as Cheyenne. He was a childless widower. After the passing of his woman he had thrown himself into land and cattle, nothing else. He couldn't have succeeded as well as he had unless he had been an obstinate cowman with the disposition of a Longhorn bull with a sore behind.

Lefler kept three riders year around and hired another three for seasonal work. It was a matter of conjecture how many cattle he ran and if the truth were known he himself probably could not have come up with anything but a rough estimate.

His buildings were well maintained — he did not believe in having his hired hands idling. Trees he had planted years earlier from slips were now huge and shadowed much of the yard.

The main house was made of logs as were the three-sided smithy, the bunkhouse and other outbuildings.

It was the custom in windy country to put buildings in a swale; Jonas Lefler had his buildings in open country with

12

excellent visibility for miles. He did not like wind but he'd be damned if he'd let it drive him down off the open plain.

As the sheriff and his deputy approached the yard, two dogs raised Cain and propped him up. A stocky man with a flour-sack apron emerged from the bunkhouse with a long two-tined fork in one hand and a greasy towel in the other. Like the liveryman in town this individual avoided shaving.

He recognized the visitors even before he was able to discern the badges they wore, put two fingers in his mouth and whistled loudly enough to be heard well beyond the yard.

Sheriff Corning wagged his head as a man emerged from the main house, stood like a statue on the covered porch, and the bunkhouse cook went back inside.

Corning crossed the yard at a dead walk, swung down and looped his reins at the tierack. His deputy did the same thing. The lined, weathered, sinewy older man on the porch said, 'Good day to you, gents,' and gestured toward chairs in overhang shade.

Sheriff Corning dreaded what he anticipated, nevertheless he wasted no time when he said, 'Mister Lefler, you know Rufe Kelly?'

The older man nodded without taking his eyes off the sheriff.

Corning looked out over the yard, did not take one of the chairs and said, 'Rufe found some buried hides with a Circle L brand on 'em.'

Lefler sat down before speaking. 'Where?'

'That don't matter,' the sheriff replied. 'The lynching's got to stop.'

Lefler looked up. 'You tell me some damned squatter butchered two of my cattle an' in the same breath tell me I can't do justice about it?'

The lawmen remained standing. The dogs had disappeared and a puny spindrift of smoke arose from the stove pipe at the bunkhouse.

Corning's heart wasn't into this. He said, 'They butcher your cattle because they're starvin' an' you go night-ridin' and hang 'em. Mister Lefler you put me in a hell of a predicament. I taken an oath to uphold the law.'

The old man continued to squint upward from his chair. 'Al, you know the difference between justice an' the law? I'll spell it out for you. Them stump-jumpers steal my animals an' butcher 'em. By the code of justice I grew up with an' the kind we operate by in this territory, rustlers get hung. Your kind of law is in books written by fee lawyers back East somewhere that never owned a cow nor had one stole from 'em. Al, you're old enough. You know how justice has been served, and damned well, since this country was founded. You tell me which of those unwashed sons of bitches butchered two of my critters an' I'll hang 'em sure as you're standin' there.'

Rufe Kelly, silent until now, said, 'Mister Lefler, law or no law you can't go around hangin' people.'

'Deputy, you ever have livestock stole from you? No, I didn't think so.' Lefler arose. 'We can talk until the cows come home an' nothing's goin' to change. You gents ride around moanin' and wringin' your hands and me'n the other folks as is losing livestock to that railroad scum, will hang every one we can find who's been stealin' an' killin' our animals.'

Sheriff Corning looked the cowman in the eye as he said, 'We'll find the lynchers, Mister Lefler, and when a circuit riding judge comes around, we'll charge 'em with murder.'

The older man considered Corning a long moment before speaking. 'Don't get your back up with me, Al. I led the ranchers in support of you. I don't think you ought to come out here to lay down the law to me. You think about it. G'day gents.'

The ride back was even more silent than the ride out had been, and the wind had died. Shortly before entering town, Sheriff Corning said, 'It's goin' to take the army, Rufe.'

His deputy had been pondering something different. 'The old bastard'll try an' find out who hid the hides off his critters an' if he finds out there'll be another lynchin' maybe tomorrow night or the night after.'

Corning disagreed. 'He can't find out that fast, Rufe.'

The deputy looked over at his companion. 'He can find out. I'd bet new money that's how he found out other times. Ride to one of them soddies and offer ten dollars for the information he'd need. Folks livin' in half underground rat-hole soddies with hungry kids and a skinny woman would do a lot for ten dollars.'

The sheriff was silent after they had left their animals with the liveryman and went up to the jail-house, but as he dropped his hat on the desk he said, 'Rufe, I got four deputies.

They can night-ride as well as the cowmen.'

Kelly dropped down in a chair considering the sheriff and shook his head.

2

Defiance

Retaliation didn't take long. Sheriff Corning was summoned before the town council. There were six councilmen, one was owner of the Palace saloon, two owned general stores, another one was the laconic scarecrow of a liveryman and the sixth member was Reverend Joe Sitwell of the Southern Baptist congregation.

He was the councilman who opened the meeting with charges against the sheriff. Sitwell was a curly-headed man in his thirties. He was from Kentucky and sounded like it when he talked.

He told Corning cattle interests were dissatisfied with the sheriff's performance and Corning considered the clergyman from an impassive face.

It hadn't taken long for Jonas Lefler to come to town.

The clergyman leaned on his table with clasped hands considering the larger and older man wearing the badge. 'They don't like you taking the part of the squatters against cattle interests, Sheriff.'

Corning replied in a dry tone. 'What they don't like, gents, is the law going after cow-interest lynchers.'

The minister asked a question. 'Have you caught any lynchers, Sheriff?'

'No sir. They're night-riders. Show up late, kick in the door, haul a squatter out an' hang him. Sometimes they also burn 'em out and shoot their animals.' Corning paused to look around. He had the attention of his listeners. 'Gents, you hired me on to take an oath to uphold the law. Yestiddy, Rufe Kelly an' I rode out to see Jonas Lefler. He made it real plain: any squatter he finds who has killed a range cow he will hang. He said the law can go to hell or words like that. He does things accordin' to an older law. It's called justice.

'Gents, you can fire me. In a way I hope you do because as sure as I'm standin' here there's going to be a war between the cowmen an' the squatters. Now then, I either uphold the law or I don't. The cowmen don't intend to abide by the law, and I'll tell you straight out, I'm between a rock an' a hard place . . . Fire me, gents. I'll ride on an' you can handle what's comin' as sure as Gawd made sour apples.'

For a long moment there was silence before a plump man named Arthur Fleming spoke. He owned one of the two mercantile businesses in Laramie. 'Sheriff, if you ride roughshod over the stockmen you might want to figure it'll play hell with business in town. They'll go to some other town.'

Corning sat silent, gazing at the plump man until Fleming said, 'Well?'

The sheriff spoke quietly and slowly. 'I'm not a storekeeper. As far as I know what you said don't have anythin' to do with what we've been talking about.'

Fleming reddened, held his mouth tight and looked for support among the other councilmen. The next man to speak was the Baptist minister. 'The sheriff's right, Arthur. We're not talking about businesses in town, we're talking about . . .'

'I know what you're talking about,' Fleming interrupted to say. 'And you better figure how the town's goin' to prosper if Corning starts a range war.'

That was too much for the laconic liveryman. 'I don't see him startin' no war, Arthur. I see the railroad's responsible if anyone is. And what does the sheriff do; uphold the law like we hired him to do, or — what!'

Fleming reddened again and clamped his mouth tight. For the balance of the meeting he would not say a word but it could be expected that he kept up a hell of a thinking.

When the meeting adjourned although Sheriff Corning may have forcibly stated his position and the council's predicament, the councilmen ignored him as they left the fire hall. Council meetings were held upstairs.

When he got back to the jailhouse it was empty, the hanging lamp hadn't been lighted and the place was chilly. None of these things did anything to raise his spirit.

He trudged up to his room at the hotel and had kicked out of his boots, draped his sidearm and shellbelt from the back of a chair and was scratching his head when someone knocked on the door. He opened it in his stockinged feet. His caller was Deputy Rufe Kelly and he entered the room without even nodding. After the door had been closed Kelly said, 'There's a dead one outside in a squatter wagon,' and sat down.

Corning perched on the edge of his bunk, waiting.

'A feller named Dunning brought him in.'

'Lunched?'

Kelly nodded his head.

'Tonight, Rufe?'

Kelly inclined his head a second time. 'Dunning heard riders pass his place an hour or so after night-fall. He was scairt of going outside but from the sound he said it was maybe four or five riders. They were heading for the Snelling place, about a halfmile south. After he couldn't no longer hear the riders he took his rifle an' went outside. His dog was raising hell. Dunning heard a commotion down near the Snelling place.'

'He went down there?'

Rufe Kelly got a pained expression on his face. He sarcastically said, 'No, Sheriff, he didn't go down there. Like I said, he was scairt pee-less.'

'Then how'd he find the one that got hanged?'

'Snelling's woman come screamin' an' yellin' to the Dunning place. She'd been hit in the face an' was bleeding. He took her ... do you know Dunning?'

Corning was unsure whether he did

or nor. When his reply was not forthcoming Rufe Kelly arose and jerked his head.

There was a new moon and an ankle-high skiff of a chilly wind. The man sitting hunched on the wagon seat neither looked around when the lawmen approached his wagon nor spoke. He sat up there and even by nightfall was an epitome of dejection.

Rufe leaned. 'You recognize him, Al?'

Corning did, but remembered him only as someone he'd seen a few times in town. Rufe jutted his jaw. Corning leaned closer to see the rope marks. The man on the wagon seat still neither looked around nor moved, but he spoke. 'That's enough. I got a wife an' a girl. Suppose they hadn't ridden past . . . '

Sheriff Corning leaned far enough to remove the contents of the corpse's pockets and straighten back. He asked about the widow and as before the slumped figure answered in an inflectionless voice without looking around.

'My wife's lookin' after her.'

'What did she say?'

'She was hysterical, Sheriff, she didn't make sense when she spoke. She was shakin' like a leaf.' Finally the slumped silhouette turned. Corning was sure he had seen the man before but could not at the moment recall where he had seen him or under what circumstances.

'It was rangemen, I can tell you that.'

'How do you know?' Corning asked.

'Who else, Sheriff? They've lynched other settlers. They've burnt out more. By Gawd if they want this miserable land as far as I'm concerned they can have it. What do you want me to do with *him*?'

Corning didn't answer the squatter, he addressed Rufe Kelly. 'Take him up to Doc's shed, put him on the table up there. No need to get Doc out of bed.'

Corning faced half around to speak

to the squatter, 'Ask around, see who else heard riders.'

The squatter snorted. 'No one'll have heard nor seen anything. You know that as well as I do.'

The sheriff spoke again to his deputy. 'Come back, Rufe,' he said, 'I'll be at the jailhouse,' returned to his room, sank down in the only chair and did not reach for his gun-belt nor his boots for several minutes.

He had lighted the jailhouse's hanging lamp and was putting kindling into the little iron stove when Deputy Kelly walked in, sat down, watched the older man get a fire going then spoke. 'Doc heard the commotion in the alley and came out. He wasn't happy an' after he examined the squatter he was downright mad. He held the lamp for me to look close. He said the squatter'd been in a fight an' showed me the bruised knuckles. Al, the feller who brought him in, Dunning, said there's talk among the squatters about this's gone on long enough. They're goin' to kill a rangeman for every attack on them an' theirs.'

Sheriff Corning sat down and rubbed his eyes. When he finished he said, 'Gawddammit, Rufe!'

Kelly nodded slightly. 'I second that. How'd you make out with the councilmen?'

'I told 'em to fire me because whether they do or not they're goin' to have a war on their hands . . . That push-gut Fleming said it'd be hard on business.'

Rufe Kelly gazed unwavering at the sheriff. 'If they fire you an' come to me to take the job, when I'm through talkin' they wouldn't touch me with a hunnert-foot pole. Bad for business?'

Corning leaned on the desk with hands clasped. 'If those squatters fight back . . . we'll have the war for a damned fact.'

'I told that to Dunning. He said better to die fightin' than to wait to be hung. He's goin' to load his wagon an' leave.'

'Did he say any names of the squatters that'll fight?'

'I asked him an' he just smiled at me.' The deputy went to warm his backside at the stove. 'You want to go huntin' for lynchers in the morning?'

Corning remained gazing at his clasped hands when he replied, 'All of us, Rufe. You'n me and the other deputies.'

'Where do you figure to start?'

'With that dead feller's woman. If she got hit she sure as hell saw who hit her.' The sheriff raised his eyes. 'We got to have identification.'

Rufe Kelly was not naturally cynical but he was this night. 'You heard what Dunning said. It'll be unlikely they'll identify anyone.'

'I'm bankin' on the deadman's widow. What's she got to lose that she ain't already lost?'

Corning shot up to his feet, dropped on his hat and blew out the lamp, closed the stove's damper and held the door for his deputy to precede him out into the chilly night.

The following morning Doctor Loomis appeared at the jailhouse only moments after Sheriff Corning had crossed from the café to his office.

Leslie Loomis was not a tall man but he was muscular. He was also short-tempered and when he wanted to be, downright gruff. He was beginning to grey at the temples. When he walked in, the sheriff gestured toward a chair, and sat down at his desk, which was actually an oversized kitchen table.

Doctor Loomis wasted no time on the customary pleasantries. He said, 'I can tell you how that squatter died.'

'Got lynched,' Corning laconically stated.

'He got yanked up by a man on a horse with dallies around the horn who jumped out his horse to yank the squatter up. He broke the man's neck. That's what killed him. The hang rope was incidental. Sheriff, those night riders are barbarians.'

Corning said, 'Amen. Anything else, Doc?'

'The squatter was in a fist fight. He took a few hits; I can show you the black-and-blue places. I can show you something else. I got it here in my pocket.' He withdrew a silver locket and tossed it on the sheriff's desk as he said, 'Open it.'

There were two miniature pictures inside, one of a smiling man the other of a young woman. She was also smiling.

Corning closed the locket and raised his eyes. 'Is that all, because me'n my deputies got some ridin' to do.'

As the medical man arose and went to the door he said, 'An eye for an eye, Sheriff?' Did not await an answer and closed the door after himself.

Al Corning left the office door open and when his deputies arrived he was curt and brief. 'Saddle guns, lads an' maybe some jerky or chittlins. It might be a long ride.'

None of the deputies asked questions; they didn't have to, they'd heard about the dead squatter and the sheriff's reaction.

As the five of them rode northward out of town, watchers from doorways and windows wasted little time in conjecturing. The conjecturing favoured a manhunt for stockmen. Although they relied largely for their bread and butter from cattle interests, they had heard of the latest killing about the time the roosters crowed. Places like Laramie had an excellent moccasin telegraph.

At the Palace saloon the barman who operated the place for an absentee owner, whose name was Mark Turner, picked up and disseminated more gossip that even the local Ladies Altar Society of the Baptist Church had not heard.

He watched the lawmen leave town looking over the top of his spindle doors and when a local idler ambled up the barman turned, smiled and said,

'They're going after bear this time.'

It was a good guess and until the sheriff and his deputies returned, the twin mills of gossip and conjecture would work overtime.

A rangeman who had come to town for the mail and half a wagonload of supplies watched the lawmen leave town from behind the roadway window of Arthur Fleming's emporium.

He left town with his laden spring wagon, drove at a walk until he was a mile out, then whistled up the horse into a gallop.

There was no sign of the lawmen. They had left the road following wagon tracks and eventually arrived at the Dunning place where a number of scrawny chickens scattered at the approach of horsemen and an old dog came from some shady place to bark his warning and his challenge.

There was no barn but there was a three-sided shed with a stanchion for a milk cow and a tie-stall for a horse. There were no trees but the porch of the house had a rude overhang. The house itself was no more than was minimally required. It had looked new five years earlier, now it looked warped and faded.

A man Rufus Kelly and the sheriff recognized came out to stand on the porch watching the lawmen tie up, loosen cinches and scuff dust in the direction of the house.

The squatter had benches but no chairs, he invited the lawmen to be seated. He had no whiskey but he had spring water. None of the lawmen were thirsty. Corning asked where the widow woman was and Dunning jerked his head. 'Inside. My wife's with her. Sheriff, she isn't in good shape.'

Corning acknowledged that with a silent nod. He hadn't ridden this far to favour a woman's indisposition. He said, 'We'd like to talk to her.'

'Well, Sheriff . . . '

'*Now!*'

Dunning went inside and returned in minutes escorting a greying woman

34

with a swollen jaw and an eye that was pinched nearly closed.

She went to a bench, sat, and with both hands clasped in her lap looked at the sheriff. Some of her facial swelling was the result of crying, but when Corning told her who he was and who his deputies were, she nodded. She already knew who the sheriff was. She'd seen him in Laramie several times.

'Ma'am, we'd like you to tell us what happened last night.'

She spoke in a voice as dry as old corn husks without looking at any of them. 'We was in bed. Someone beat on the door. I told my husband not to go, but he went . . . They grabbed him . . .'

'How many, ma'am?'

'Five. I ran at one of them. He had my husband's arm twisted far up his back. I run at him, kicked and scratched and he hit me in the face. I . . .'

'Would you recognize him?' the sheriff asked.

'I'd recognize him an' the redheaded one who was on a horse. They tied a rag over my husband's mouth, tied his hands in back. I was beginnin' to come round on the ground when the redheaded man hooked his horse so hard it jumped six, eight feet and lit down running. He set it up real hard . . . I fainted, Sheriff. When I come round . . . ' The woman's resolve was breaking.

Dunning's wife came out glaring. She was made of something different than her husband; she said, 'Sheriff, get on your horse and get out of this yard. What have you done? They kill our men and what have you done? Where we come from they'd tie you to a tree and whip your back raw. *Get!*'

Her husband was embarrassed. He waited until the two women had gone inside before saying, 'She won't leave. I talked to her last night. She says we got legal right to stay and we'll stay.'

Sheriff Corning arose, offered his hand, led his deputies to the horses, mounted up and left the yard in a slow walk.

The youngest deputy, a former rangeman, said, 'Lefler's top hand is redheaded.'

No one commented, the youngest deputy rode in silence as did his companions. When they reached the coach road, the sheriff didn't turn southward toward town, he crossed the road and kept on riding.

Rufe looked sharply at him. 'Lefler's got six hands,' he said, and might as well have been talking to a stone wall.

It was a fairly long ride and the day was better than half spent when they came to a willow-lined creek.

The sheriff swung down, loosened the cinch, removed the bridle and led his horse to water. The others followed his example. While they were doing this someone made a shrill whistle. Whoever had done it was invisible but when they snugged up and rebridled their horses Rufe spoke to the sheriff.

'It's not going to be a surprise.'

The sheriff nodded without speaking and led the others across the creek. They had jerky but only the youngest rider chewed it.

When they had the buildings in sight the sheriff said, 'I want that redheaded son of a bitch. If the old man wants to fight, fine.'

Whether the deputies felt the same way or not, none of them spoke but the older ones yanked loose the tie-down thongs over their holstered sidearms.

A dog barked while the law-riders were still a considerable distance from the yard. No one appeared in the yard, at the bunkhouse or the main house. The youngest deputy spoke hopefully. 'This time of day more'n likely they're lookin' for sorefooted bulls or maybe hung-up first-calf heifers.'

An older man tapped his arm and shook his head. The younger man freed up his holstered Colt as the others had done and did not say another word.

Sheriff Corning led them into the yard, scuffing dust as far as the tie rack out front of the barn.

3

A Dazzling Bright Light

Jonas Lefler came out on to his veranda. He was not wearing a sidearm but the four men who came out behind him were.

Corning told Rufe and the others to wait, crossed to the steps and said, 'Good day, Jonas.'

The squinty-eyed older man responded the same way, 'Good morning, Sheriff.' It was afternoon, which mattered not at all.

'Jonas, I'm looking for a redheaded rangeman.'

'Are you now? What's his name?'

Corning had no idea what the man's name was. 'I got no idea. Do you have a redheaded rider?'

The older man did not speak, he slowly shook his head. One of the

40

men behind him cleared his throat. He and his companions were watching the deputies down with their horses.

The sheriff spoke again, still in a mild tone of voice. 'Night-riders lynched a squatter named Snelling last night and hit his woman. One of 'em was redheaded. Jonas, you're shy two riders.'

'They're out with the cattle,' Lefler replied. 'Don't either of 'em have red hair . . . Sheriff?'

Corning nodded.

'Did that hanged squatter have butchered beef in his house?'

'I didn't go to his house, Jonas. I talked to his widow at a neighbour's house.'

'Feller named Dunning?'

'Yes.'

'He's been troublesome, Sheriff.'

'He wants to leave the country . . . Jonas, there's something else: they're fixin' to fight back.'

Lefler was expressionless. 'Are they for a fact? You better tell 'em that wouldn't be a good idea.'

One of the rangemen behind Lefler raised his head staring. Down at the hitch rack the deputies were also looking northward.

Two horsemen were approaching in a lope. One of the men with Jonas Lefler let his breath out in an audible sigh. The riders hauled down to a walk as they entered the yard, saw the men wearing badges, saw the men at the front of the house and one rider spun his horse and ran it belly-down back the way he had come.

Rufe Kelly called from the tie rack, 'Redheaded, Al.'

Corning called back, 'Run him down, Rufe. I want the son of a bitch alive.'

As the deputies mounted and whirled in pursuit, a tall, darkly tanned rangeman to one side of Jonas Lefler said, 'They'll never catch him. He's mounted on the fastest horse we got.'

Sheriff Corning looked steadily at the rancher. 'They're out with the cattle,

Jonas, an' don't either of 'em have red hair?'

Lefler returned the lawman's gaze with a hard stare. 'I hire 'em to work. I don't go round lookin' at their hair.'

'Jonas, you know what obstructing the law means?'

Lefler's gaze remained cold. 'You going to take me in, Sheriff? You're goin' to get yourself buried if you try it.'

From the direction of a low landswell someone whistled. It was a loud sound and carried well.

Sheriff Corning twisted to look toward the landswell. As he did this Lefler said, 'You want to take me in, Al?'

Horsemen appeared atop the landswell, nine of them spaced out and unmoving. The distance was too great for the horsemen to be identified but that wasn't really necessary. The distance wasn't so great it wasn't possible to see that the stationary horsemen had booted Winchesters under their *rosaderos*.

Lefler wasn't smiling but he was smug. 'Al . . . ?'

Corning faced back around. 'Jonas, I'm trying to avoid a war. You'n your friends up yonder aren't makin' it easy for me.'

'A war? Who with, them squatting bastards on our range? Let 'em start it.'

Sheriff Corning looked briefly at the older man with his expression of unrelenting hostility, turned, went down to the tie rack, mounted and left the yard in a steady walk.

Before he was beyond hearing, someone on the porch made a scornful laugh.

He rode all the way back to town, let the liveryman care for his animal, went to the café, had supper and crossed to the jailhouse to light the hanging lamp, sit down and wait.

Rufe and a deputy named Horace King came in to dust off and drop on to benches. King was a tall man in his thirties. He had a reputation for being soft-spoken, tough and fearless. He spoke before Rufe Kelly did.

'We never more'n got a glimpse of him. If he wasn't ridin' a thoroughbred race horse I'm a monkey's uncle.'

Rufe added to it. 'He run south-west. Like Horace said, we didn't have a horse that could put us within shootin' distance.'

Sheriff Corning mused aloud. 'South-west; that'd be in the direction of the Moran place.'

Rufus nodded; he was tired, thirsty and hungry and his lower back was giving him hell.

Peter Moran was a close friend of Jonas Lefler. He was a large, forceful individual whose prosperity had encouraged a latent bullying nature to become overt. If the redheaded lyncher had run for it in the direction of the Moran place he would certainly be put up and his animal cared for.

The sheriff didn't have the heart to

45

take Rufe and Horace King on a long night-ride, they were worn down. He said, 'You did your best. Go get fed and bed down. I'm obliged to you both.'

Rufe was watching Corning. When the sheriff finished speaking Rufus Kelly said, 'What're you going to do?'

'Well; on a rested-up fast horse that murdering son of a bitch can leave the country in the morning, which means we might never see him again.'

Rufe pushed out tired legs. 'So you figure to ride down there tonight?'

'Rufe, you boys go eat an' bed down.'

As the pair of deputies went to the door Rufe looked back. 'You'll get yourself killed. By now, Lefler an' as many of his friends as he can round up will be all over the range. They'll track you to the Moran place and . . . Good night, Sheriff. One more word, they're used to night-riding.'

With the door closed at their back the deputies spoke briefly before parting.

Horace had said, 'He'll start the damned war, Rufe. Good night.'

As Rufe walked the dark and empty roadway in the direction of the rooming-house where he stayed, he had a bitter thought. If Horace King was right, the sheriff was going to start the damned war he wanted to prevent. If there was irony in that Rufe missed it.

Horace's idea had merit and Rufe Kelly's premonition, although justified, overlooked a salient factor: Alfred Corning had grown long in the tooth in the lawman's occupation.

He knew more ways to skunk trackers and manhunters than folks could shake a stick at.

Corning went about what he had to do without enthusiasm. It rankled that he'd been made to eat crow earlier in the day at the Lefler place but he could live with that if he could find and apprehend that redheaded lyncher.

If the lyncher wasn't at the Moran place, Corning would have a long ride back to town. If he was there; something else he had learned over the years was that one man in the right place at the right time could often prove more likely to succeed than a company of soldiers.

He left town by the alley behind the livery barn where a dim-witted night hostler watched him depart before returning to the harness room to sleep.

There was a sickle moon in a vast curving sky whose darkness was punctuated by bright little stars. It was warm most of the way but that wouldn't deter anyone who'd spent much time in the north country; it could turn cold in minutes.

Peter Moran and Jonas Lefler shared overlapping grasslands. At the autumn gather they co-operated. There was an age difference of something like ten or fifteen years, something neither cowman considered. If there was a personal difference it was that Jonas Lefler, hard as iron, made no statement he wasn't prepared to back up, and he did it in a quiet tone of voice.

Peter Moran was large, powerful and financially well off. There was no way to determine if he'd been a bully as a child but he was known in the Laramie country as a bully in his later years.

By the time Sheriff Corning could make out rooftops and old trees in a wide, low swale, the moon had shifted considerably.

There were no lights; because the hour was late there wouldn't be. There were dogs but they seemed only half-heartedly hostile, possibly because they had been roused from their beds at the scent of a horseman approaching from the north-east.

Corning entered the yard without haste, the worrisome yammering of dogs increased as he looped his reins at the tie rack out front of the barn, entered the building which was twice as dark inside as the night was outside, and went along the stalls on both sides of the runway. There were four stalls on each side. Three were occupied by horses who opened heavy eyes and regarded Corning irritably.

One horse poked its head over the lower half of the stall door. Corning chummed his way up to it speaking softly. The horse did not turn its rump nor back deeper into the stall. Corning ran a bare hand down the animal's neck on the right side. It was damp. Corning went inside the stall and did the same thing down the horse's back and encountered more sweat-warmth. Visibility was too poor for a real assessment of the horse but with eyes adjusting to the gloom Corning stood back.

The horse was between fifteen and sixteen hands tall, had well-muscled forearms. If it wasn't a purebred running horse it was a good imitation.

Corning went out, latched the stall, was beginning to turn when a brilliant white light blinded him.

Two hours later, with the sun coming, Corning groped for something to lean on as he arose, used the stall door for that purpose at about the same time a splitting headache arrived in full force.

He leaned on the stall door. The horse inside was eating hay from a corner manger. Corning could hear his grinders working.

He felt weak and ill. His hat was on the ground. There was a trickle of blood from a growing lump where his hat had been. He instinctively felt for his holstered Colt. It was in place but the tie-down thong hung loose.

There was not a sound in the yard. Even the dogs had given up and crawled back under the porch of the main house.

When the sheriff went to the wide front opening, sunlight hit his eyes like hot iron. He retreated as far as an empty horseshoe keg near a saddle pole and sat down, wiped watering eyes with a blue bandanna and leaned back.

He'd had headaches before from too much whiskey, from bumps, from being jumped off bucking horses, but never with the sickening intensity of this headache.

There was a quick cure but he was a long ride from the medicine man in Laramie who could dispense it.

He explored the lump. It was nearly half the size of a man's fist and although the blood had clotted with his hair, the slightest touch made him lock his jaws.

He sat a long while, nothing happened, no one appeared and there was no noise.

The pain did not diminish except to gradually become a sullen kind of ache. He went out back to the trough, soaked his face and head, which helped, considered the corralled using horses as they also considered him, and soaked his head a second time. Each time he did this his vision improved, the ache lessened a little, and someone walking in the barn caught and held his attention. he turned.

A grinning rangeman who was

ordinary in every way except one, he had a shock of unshorn red hair, said, 'A man had ought to know better'n try to steal a horse out of someone's barn in the night, Sheriff.'

Corning eased down on the damp edge of the trough. He had probably seen the rangeman before, in town or on the range, but for the life of him he couldn't recall any such meeting.

The grinning man leaned in the doorway. 'You're lucky Mister Moran had to go look at some sick cows his riders found yestiddy. He'd've hung you. Mister Moran's a man who don't like horsethieves.'

Corning finally spoke; he still had the ache but the pain was about half gone. He said, 'You got a name, Red?'

The grin widened. 'That's it.'

'Red what?'

This time the grinning redhead gave a delayed reply. 'Mister, where you're goin', far as I know they don't use names.' He palmed his six-gun without haste and nodded. 'Stand up, Mister

Corning. Face to face. Good. Now then, I'm goin' to leather my pistol an' it'll be an even shootout. You ready, Mister Corning?'

A voice the sheriff recognized said, 'Redhead, you touch that pistol an' I'll blow your head off! *Drop it!* Real careful. *I said drop it!*'

The grinning rangeman's expression smoothed out. He started to turn and was given a curt order. 'Don't move, you son of a bitch. Two seconds — *Drop it!*'

The rangeman lifted out his Colt and let it fall. The man Sheriff Corning could not see well in the barn gloom, now addressed him.'

'Lift out your gun, Sheriff. Now then, open the cap an' turn the cylinder.'

Corning did as he'd been told, spun the cylinder and raised his eyes to the redheaded man. 'Empty,' he said, and the rangeman neither moved nor spoke.

The man behind him in barn shadow said, 'Take his belt, tie his wrists behind his back. Sheriff, you deaf?'

Corning returned his empty sidearm to its holster, stepped in front of the rangeman, yanked the belt loose of its loops, turned the rangeman roughly and drew the belt tightly enough to squeeze off circulation, then he shoved the rangeman in front of him and entered the barn.

'*Rufe!*'

The man in shadows answered with heavy sarcasm. 'Who'd you expect, the Tooth Fairy? Sheriff . . . forget it, let's get this lynching bastard on a horse an' get the hell out of here.'

The thoroughbred horse needed water so Corning let him tank up at the trough before saddling it with the only saddle on the pole.

Rufe Kelly led in the other two animals, handed Corning his reins and said, 'Your horse's been standin' out at that tie rack all night. He's shrunk up like a gutted snow bird. Let's go.'

They were leaving the yard when

three dogs appeared. Two watched the riders with wagging tails. A younger dog barked for all he was worth.

Rufe said, 'That ought to rouse 'em. Let's make tracks.'

As the three men loped, the rangeman said, 'Ain't no one back there. They got sick cows.'

The sheriff looked at the man whose horse he was leading. 'One more time: what's your name?'

'Red Hewlett.'

'You got a first name?'

The rangeman did not meet the sheriff's gaze when he answered, 'Amaryllis.'

Even Rufe twisted to gaze at the redheaded man. 'What in hell's that mean?'

Amaryllis Hewlett was red in the face when he replied, 'I don't know what it means. My ma hung it on me. I think it's some kind of flower.'

Nothing more was said until they had town in sight. The sheriff leaned and addressed the rangeman. 'You

56

should've traded horses an' kept on goin'.'

'I figured to before sunrise. That's how I come up behind you.'

Rufe twisted again, 'Amaryllis, they don't call you that, do they?'

'They been callin' me Red since I can remember.'

'Red, did Jonas Lefler pay you extra for lynchin' that squatter named Snelling?'

'What are you talkin' about? I didn't lynch no one.'

'His wife can identify you. Amaryllis, which one of you fellers hit the woman in the face?'

The rangeman looked steadily at Rufe Kelly without opening his mouth and that's how they crossed the west-side alley behind the livery barn.

When the liveryman came to take their reins, saw blood and a trussed rider, his eyes popped so wide a person could have straddled one eyeball and sawed off the other one.

Rufe growled when the liveryman

would have spoke. He went to work on the animals as the pair of lawmen herded their prisoner up to the jailhouse where Rufe pushed him down on a bench and the rangeman complained. He couldn't sit back with both arms cinched in back. Rufe said, 'Sit back anyway,' and faced the sheriff. 'I knew you'd do somethin' like that.'

Corning said, 'Lock him up, I'm goin' up to the doc's place.'

Rufe leaned for a closer look at the sheriff's head. 'What'd he hit you with, a tree?'

After the sheriff had left, Rufe herded the rangeman to one of the cages in the cell room, removed the belt and tossed it on the floor, went outside, locked the steel door and said, 'For a plugged *centavo* I'd've shot you.'

With steel straps between them the rangeman sneered, 'Deputy, when Mister Lefler hears about this you better be miles away.'

Rufe returned to the office, slammed the cellroom door after himself, tossed the key ring on the desk, tipped back his hat and silently swore.

That he'd probably saved the sheriff's life only barely balanced out against the loss of sleep he'd sacrificed, and he'd been dog-tired before his conscience had prodded him to go after that pig-headed damned fool, when anyone with the sense Gawd gave a goose would know riding to the Moran place alone was an invitation to an early grave.

4

Taking the Initiative

It was a persistent bump, which hadn't required stitching and Doc Loomis had said whoever had hit the sheriff could have accomplished his purpose with half the force.

He gave the sheriff some white pills, told him if the pain persisted to come back and he'd give him some stronger pain killers.

Sheriff Corning was rarely without a hat; from this time forward he even wore his hat in the jailhouse office.

The little pills deadened all pain for about two hours, after which he took another one.

He ached from weariness but otherwise after a big breakfast he felt fit.

He brought the redheaded rangeman to his office, sat him down and said,

'If the circuit rider's Sam Potts . . . he hates lynchers.'

Amaryllis Hewlett looked neither fearful nor impressed. He said, 'Are you layin' a charge on me, Sheriff?'

'Murder.'

Hewlett made a faint, humourless smile. 'You got any idea who you're goin' up against?'

Corning nodded. 'Pete Moran for hidin' a fugitive an' Jonas Lefler for aidin' and abettin' one.'

Hewlett made a laugh that sounded like pieces of steel rubbing together which the sheriff ignored. 'I know you killed that squatter. What you're goin' to tell me is the name of the man who hit his wife in the face.'

Red Hewlett looked straight at the sheriff when he said, 'I'm goin' to tell you nothin'; Mister Lefler'll do the talkin' for me.'

Corning sat gazing at his prisoner for over an interlude of silence before saying, 'I owe you for cold-cocking me in the barn. I'll square things between us.' Corning arose. 'Get up.'

He locked the rangeman back in his cell and returned to his office, draped the key ring from its wall peg, sat down and had his thoughts interrupted when Horace King walked in looking fresh and shaved. He said, 'I saw Rufe across the road. Hell, I'd have rode out there last night with you. What'd Red have to say?'

'Nothing. He's countin' on Jonas Lefler.'

The rawboned deputy went to a bench and sat down as he said, 'Lefler's in town with his riders. They were at the eatery. Sheriff, I'll go round up the other fellers.'

Corning gingerly shook his head. 'Let it go for now.'

'Sure as hell Lefler'll come here.'

The sheriff gently inclined his head. 'I hope he does. Horace, later on you can round 'em up. We'll ride to the Moran place. That's where Red Hewlett was waitin' for morning before heading out.'

Horace King nodded as he arose from the bench. 'I'll find the fellers an' tell 'em.'

After Horace King had left the office, Corning's prisoner began rattling his strap-steel cage. Corning ignored him, went to stand by the only small, grilled roadway window and gazed in the direction of the saloon. Normally, this early in the day, Mark Turner had few patrons. This morning the tie rack out front had five or six horses tethered there.

Corning went back to his desk. Hewlett was no longer yelling. He hadn't been fed this morning.

Rufe Kelly came in out of a cloudless sun-bright day. With no preliminaries he said, 'They're up at the Palace. Lefler and his riders.'

Corning's reply was dry. 'I never knew Jonas needed Dutch courage.'

Rufe dropped into a chair. 'He don't, Sheriff. Not that old devil.'

'He'll be along, Rufe.'

'Sure he will; that's part of his idea,

let folks see him'n his riders so's word'll get back to you, an' you'll sweat.'

The sheriff returned to his desk, leaned with both hands clasped and spoke quietly. 'Horace was by a while back.'

'I know. I talked to him.'

'Well, you'n Horace get the others, get shotguns an' stand over inside of Fleming's store.'

Rufe arose nodding. He didn't like it but without much doubt the range cattlemen who had been ruling the Laramie Plains since old Red Cloud was chased off would be willing to start a war. More than willing; any challenge to their overlordship would make them eager to settle in their way the simmering hostility that had been accumulating since the railroad people had first appeared to squat — legally or not — on land two generations of stockmen claimed.

At the door Rufe said, 'Al, this isn't no way to prevent it. This is how to start it.'

Corning repeated his earlier statement. 'Shotguns over in front of the emporium, Rufe. I'm not goin' to start it. Lefler already has an' I got the proof in the cell room.'

Rufe departed to begin his search for the other deputies. His expression was as grim as what he told the deputies when he located them, and Rufe led them down to Fleming's store and inside where, over the red-faced sputtering words of Arthur Fleming they took every shotgun from his gun rack, requisitioned boxes of cartridges and went to stand inside the store at the roadway window. Fleming scolded, ranted and swore, less about having his scatterguns appropriated than about what would happen when customers entered the store and saw those armed men watching the roadway.

The youngest deputy saw them first on the far-side plankwalk, Jonas Lefler in the lead, his riders following.

Horace said, 'Tie-down loose, Rufe. It'd be better if we was in the office.'

The reply he got was given in a bleak tone of voice. 'It's what the sheriff said to do.'

Corning was at his desk, hat tipped back, sorting through papers when the older man and his expressionless riders walked in. He looked up and nodded. 'Jonas . . . nice morning.'

Lefler was abrupt and brusque, 'Where's Hewlett?'

'In a cell.'

'Turn him loose, Sheriff.'

'I got a murder charge against him, Jonas. He stays locked up until a circuit rider gets here.'

Lefler scratched an unshaven jaw without taking his squinty stare off the lawman. 'I got a fee lawyer comin' from Cheyenne. We'll have Red out of here by tomorrow. You'd make it easier if you turned him loose now . . . How much bail, Sheriff?'

'A million dollars, Jonas.'

A rangeman let go a startled gasp, otherwise there was silence until the cowman spoke again. 'Al, we've known each other a long time . . . '

'Jonas, Hewlett stays. I want to have a long talk with him.'

'We can bust him out of here, Sheriff.'

Corning arose from his desk. Lefler's hired riders put their full attention on him as he walked to the little barred roadway window, gazed in silence for a moment before turning to address Lefler. 'You're right, Jonas, we've known each other a long time. Come over here, I want to show you somethin'.'

Lefler hesitated briefly before crossing to the little window. Corning had to hunch a little, which he did as he said, 'Look yonder.'

Lefler leaned, squinted hard and said, 'Look at what?'

'The window in Art Fleming's store.'

This time the cowman's squint was less hard. He did not move for a long time before he straightened and faced the sheriff. 'You're tryin' to avoid a range war? It don't look like it from here, Sheriff.'

Corning returned to his desk but did not sit down. He spoke to Lefler's rangemen. 'They're across the road with shotguns. If any of you or your boss start somethin' in here not a damned one of you'll walk away and live.'

A weathered, dark rangeman switched his eyes to Jonas Lefler. 'What's he talkin' about?'

'Four deputies over at Fleming's store with scatterguns.'

The same man's reaction wasn't surprise. He made a small grin. 'Flanked, Mister Lefler. You're a good stockman but you'd never make a good soldier. If they're behind us we been flanked.'

Sheriff Corning shouldered his way to the door and opened it as he jerked his head. 'Out! Don't even think about them holsters. *Out!*' The weathered former soldier led the exodus.

Outside, the former soldier raised his

right hand in a salute to the deputies in the store and one of them saluted back. The Circle L men went in the direction of the Palace.

Corning blocked the door so that Jonas Lefler could not follow his riders out. He said, 'Jonas, I'm goin' to prove you told Hewlett what to do an' who to lynch. You only think you're above the law. Another thing, Jonas: if there's one more lynching I'm coming after you personal. No matter who does it or sends riders to do it, an' I'm not goin' to hold you over for a circuit rider. I'm personally goin' to hang you from a tree beside the stage road. *Git!*'

Lefler walked up the centre of the road as far as the Palace. He went inside. Ten minutes later he and his riders mounted up and left town by the north roadway. It was a ruse and it worked.

Fleming got his shotguns back unused along with the cartons of shells. He was as red as a beet but said nothing until the deputies were crossing toward the jailhouse, then he swore.

Horace King was the first to enter the office, Rufe and the others trailed afterwards. Horace smiled broadly. 'Scairt the whey out of that old bastard, did you, Sheriff?'

Corning was still standing at his desk when he replied, 'That old bastard don't scare. He hadn't no choice but to listen, but gents, don't make the mistake of thinkin' you or me scairt him.'

Rufe spoke next. 'He wanted Hewlett let go?' and when the sheriff nodded Rufe also said, 'If he thinks Hewlett will tell you anythin' he'll move heaven an' earth to keep him quiet.'

No comment on Rufe's statement was required, every man in the room was aware that this was so. Only the youngest deputy had a comment to make. 'If he's worried about that, bein' the way he is, would he try to take Hewlett out maybe at gun point?'

No one answered. Horace King thought that was a far-fetched idea, but not everyone did. Sheriff Corning drank some water from a hanging *olla* and wiped his mouth on his sleeve as he returned to the desk. For the moment, Jonas Lefler's place in their palaver was taken in a fresh direction when Corning said, 'Lefler's got a fee lawyer comin' from Cheyenne. I think that'll hold him off for a spell. But Pete Moran's the feller who helped Red Hewlett hide out when you lads chased him.' Corning hesitated. During this brief interlude all the deputies watched and waited.

'I don't know how many riders Moran has, but I want his hide for aiding and abetting.'

Rufe said, 'Today?'

'No; it's a long ride. First thing in the morning.'

The youngest deputy had a question. 'Who's goin' to mind Hewlett while we're gone?'

This time the older men were thoughtful until the sheriff said, 'I've done it before. I'll weigh him down with chains an' ask Joe Sitwell to mind the place until we get back.'

He got several doubting looks but no one spoke. They all left except rawboned Horace King. He said, 'Sheriff, if they come to take Hewlett out, havin' a preacher guardin' him . . . is that a real good idea?'

Corning arose. 'If someone comes to town to bust Hewlett out an' start a fight, I think the preacher can take care of it. He can get some fellers from his congregation to help.'

The rawboned man stood staring for a moment, then burst into laughter.

After he left, the sheriff went up to the Palace which wasn't as busy as it would be after sundown. Four regulars were playing toothpick poker near a roadway window. Two had been soldiers; one was older; he'd been a buffalo hunter. The fourth poker player was a one-legged old man named Fred Sawyer. He'd owned the livery barn until he couldn't hire reliable help nor do it all himself and had sold out to the present owner.

Mark Turner served the sheriff with an expressionless face. There was no one else at the bar. Corning downed his jolt and pushed the glass for a refill. Up to this time neither man had spoken; it wasn't necessary, they were old friends, but as Turner leaned to refill the little jolt glass he softly said, 'You stuck a burr under Jonas's saddle blanket. He left here madder'n a wet hen.'

The sheriff smiled. 'I wouldn't let him have the feller who killed that last squatter.'

Turner raised his eyes. 'Al, that old man's no one to fool with.'

Again the sheriff nodded, but this time he didn't do it until he emptied the small glass, then he looked straight at Mark Turner. 'Him an' his friends want all the squatters out, burn their buildings an' tear down their fences.'

Turner knew this; he'd heard little else for months. He said, 'An' you figure to buck them?'

'Yes. You can't night-ride up to someone's house, haul 'em out an' hang 'em. That's murder, Mark.'

Turner used the damp rag tucked under his belt to make a wide sweep of the bartop. He leaned and gently shook his head. 'Al, you'n four deputies won't be enough. Jonas Lefler has six riders. The others backin' him will have maybe a total of twenty more.'

Sheriff Corning looked unblinkingly at the barman. 'Will that make them right? They'll keep it up until the squatters get enough. Then there'll be a range war.' Corning pushed away from the bar. 'That's what I want to prevent. What'll happen to your business, every other business in town, if this lynchin' business isn't stopped?'

Turner could have answered, instead he repeated what he'd said earlier. 'Buck 'em, Al, an' they'll lynch you too.'

The sheriff made that slight, humourless

smile again as he turned to depart. His final words were, 'I may have to deputize men from town. You, for example.'

He left the saloonman motionless behind his bar watching the spindle doors rocking back and forth.

The sheriff went up to his room at the hotel, shed as much as he usually did, climbed between the blankets, blew down the lamp mantle, put his arms under his head and stared into the darkness.

He had forgotten something; talking to the preacher. He would do it first thing in the morning. Damnation!

He didn't sleep well. What Turner had said was true, he was fixing to buck local stockmen, their riders, their lynching back-shooters.

When he left the bed it was still dark out. He went out back to wash up, returned to get dressed, dumped his hat on and walked out into pre-dawn chill.

There was a flicker of yellow light

up at the house behind the Baptist church, and that was encouraging. He had no idea why the minister would be up before daylight but was relieved that he was.

He walked up there leaving echoing footsteps. Even the town dogs were sleeping. When he rattled the door the shockle-headed minister opened the door with light at his back. He recognized his visitor and stepped aside as he said, 'An old man once told me folks that can't sleep until daylight have bad consciences. Care for a cup of coffee?'

Corning nodded. 'I'd like that. Joe, I need a favour.'

From where Sitwell was filling two crockery mugs at the stove he said, 'What kind of favour, Sheriff?'

'I got the rangeman who killed that squatter named Snelling in the jailhouse. Me'n my lads got to be gone most of the day.'

Sitwell set a cup on the small table between them and sat down. 'And you want me to make sure your prisoner's in his cell when you get back?'

Corning nodded while reaching for the crockery cup. 'Good guess, Joe.'

'You've come to me for this before, Sheriff. Who is your prisoner?'

'A redheaded feller named Hewlett. He rides for Jonas Lefler.'

The minister's cup froze halfway to his face. 'Does Jonas know you have him?'

'Yes. He come by yesterday, wanted Hewlett turned loose.'

'And you refused.'

'Joe, the son of a bitch killed that squatter.'

'By hanging, like the others?'

'No! He jumped out his horse, when the rope got tight it broke the squatter's neck. He's down at Doc's shed behind the house.'

Sitwell sipped coffee, slowly and carefully put the cup down as he said, 'When he's crossed Mister Lefler's bad medicine.'

'I know that. What should I do?

Twiddle my thumbs until him an' his friends lynch 'em all?'

'And if he returned to town while you're gone . . . ?'

'How many men in your congregation, Joe?'

Sitwell didn't answer for a long time, he sat gazing at the sheriff. Eventually he said, 'All right. I have about thirty regulars in the congregation. How long'll you be gone?'

'All day. Peter Moran's place is a fair distance.'

The minister considered the hands around his coffee cup. 'Moran's trouble, Sheriff. Why do you want him?'

'He hid out the redheaded Lefler rider who killed the squatter.'

'You know this for a fact?'

'I'm satisfied he's the one,' Corning said as he arose. 'Joe, don't feed him.'

The minister also arose. 'I remember you doin' this before. All right. If Mister Lefler comes to town for your prisoner he'll get a surprise . . . Al, be careful; Moran is hell on wheels.'

At the door the sheriff smiled. 'I'm obliged, Joe.'

The minister nodded without speaking and after the sheriff's departure rolled his eyes skyward.

5

Pete Moran

They met at the livery barn and under the bleary gaze of the night man who had been roused from sleep, they rigged out, buckled saddle boots holding Winchester saddle guns into place and led their animals out in the cold early morning.

The night man returned to his bedroll on the harness-room floor shaking his head.

Nothing was said for some distance until the youngest deputy stated as a fact that he'd been able to eat breakfast, something the older men did not comment about. They didn't live at home.

They were thinking of what was ahead. Moran could be expected to be truculent and defiant. If his hired riders took their cue from their employer there was going to be a fight and that mattered according to how many men the lawmen would face.

A deputy named Jed Nutting said he thought Moran had three riders, all seasonal men, which meant if they were kept on year round they would be loyal to the brand, which was not only the custom it was also a cow-country honour.

The sheriff's headache was gone and the lump on his head was diminishing. He hadn't thought of it at all today until Rufe drifted up to ride stirrup with him and asked.

Corning raised his hat, felt the lump, reset the hat and said, 'I owe that redheaded son of a bitch for that, too.'

Rufe smiled in the cold darkness. 'I'd say you two was about even. I got a feelin', Pete Moran'll fight.'

The sheriff agreed. 'I expect he will. But you can't never tell about those big-mouthed, bullyin' folks.'

They were close enough for dogs to pick up their scent and to bark. They continued to ride. Every man had his tie-down loose. The only sound was of shod horses and leather rubbing over leather where someone had neglected to oil and soap his outfit, which was not uncommon. Only saddle-makers and old ladies took care of leather and often times the old ladies let it slide.

They were close to the yard when the agitated barking incited someone in the bunkhouse to light a candle. To light the hanging lamp it was necessary to stand on a chair. Candles were handier. At least two of the dogs retreated to safety as the lawmen entered the yard, but one large, shaggy dog continued to bark and threaten while simultaneously wagging his tail.

They swung off and looped reins at the tie rack in front of the barn. The tail-wagging dog responded when Horace King leaned and held out a hand. The dog wiggled his way up to be patted on the head. Horace had just made a lifelong friend.

The sheriff and Rufe approached the bunkhouse. Behind them a deputy named Mike Sears followed. Sears was one of those individuals who rarely spoke, not even when others thought he should. He was dark, part Indian or Mex, had eyes the colour of ink and was totally loyal and reliable. He also happened to be very good with sidearms.

They were at the bunkhouse door when a tousle-headed man with bare feet and sleep-puffy eyes opened the door. He had been in the act of swinging his arms to get the suspenders holding up his britches in place when he froze.

Sheriff Corning pushed him aside. One man was propping himself up in his bed. Another man who habitually slept like the dead, softly snored.

The lawmen spread out, removing pistols from hanging shellbelts without saying a word. The 'breed roughly jerked the hard sleeper awake. The man opened his eyes and seemed not to be breathing. About a foot in front of him a swarthy black-eyed man was holding a cocked six-gun to his face. The 'breed deputy jerked his head, 'Get up! Keep your hands where I can see 'em. *I said get up!*'

The rangeman swung into a sitting position and spoke. 'You mind if I put on my pants an' boots?'

The dark man said, 'Do it, then stand up with your hands atop your head.'

Sheriff Corning looked triumphantly at his habitually disapproving deputy and Rufe looked back and shrugged. Everyone had a right to do something right now and then.

They sat the rangemen at the bunkhouse table. Two had pants on, one was attired in seasonal long underwear. None of them looked up or at each other.

Sheriff Corning went to the head of the table, holstered his pistol and said, 'We're goin' to tie an' gag you until we have Mister Moran. I hope takin' him will be this easy.'

The tousle-headed, barefoot man whose braces held up his trousers looked at the sheriff. 'You're pretty good at sneakin' up, ain't you?'

Corning nodded and the rangeman spoke again. 'Well, you ain't goin' to do as well at the main house. Mister Moran ain't up there.'

'Where is he?'

'He don't tell us when he goes an' comes. I got no idea where he went.'

'When's he coming back?'

'I don't know that neither, Sheriff.' The rangeman ran thumbs under his suspenders and made a self-satisfied little smile.

The black-eyed, menacing-appearing deputy came up behind the barefoot man, drew a boot knife, reversed it and while holding the seated man's hair, ran the cold steel across the barefooted man's gullet.

It worked. The rangeman was leaning away from the knife when he said, 'He went over to Circle L for a meetin' of cowmen.'

'When?'

'This morning after breakfast.'

The dark deputy leaned to put up his boot knife as Rufe and Horace exchanged a look. Horace said, 'Take this bunch back with us, Sheriff?'

Corning nodded, told Horace to take care of it and returned to the yard with Rufe Kelly trailing him. It was cold, a man's voice made steam. Visibility was perfect; it was also limited by darkness.

Rufe said, 'The town council's goin' to raise hell for feeding three more prisoners.'

The sheriff was irritated. There were times when Rufe's negativity annoyed him. But this time he had an answer. 'I don't figure to keep 'em. It'll be up to them. I want information, some answers. If they help me I'll give 'em some advice: collect their wages and get out of the country.'

Rufe rolled and lighted a quirly. He

said nothing as he trickled smoke. He turned when the Moran's men appeared, hands tied around their saddlehorns. The deputies with them got astride, kept two sets of leading reins and passed one set to Rufe Kelly.

A light wind arrived. It probably came off snowy peaks because it was colder than a witch's bosom.

By the time they had town in sight, the sun was half of a big orange-coloured object on the horizon, and the wind still blew.

At the livery barn the night-man was gone and the proprietor stood aside as the riders entered his runway. Wind reached down through here too, but not as strong.

The liveryman was as prudent as he'd been other times. He'd been growled into silence other times too. He said nothing as he stalled three horses and took the others out to a corral.

Rufe Kelly didn't wait for the sheriff to feed the iron stove and light it.

The wind was increasing, it made a scrabbling sound among rafter ends.

Someone howled louder than the wind. The sheriff and his deputies exchanged glances. Their prisoner had now missed four meals.

Corning kept only the rider who wore braces, had Rufe put the others in cells.

He offered the Moran rider a chew and the man accepted, eyeing the sheriff as he got the cud tucked into a cheek.

Corning wasted no time. He sat hunched at his desk as he spoke. 'How many times have you rode with the lynchers? Lie to me, mister, an' I'll lock you in the cell with that feller who keeps yelling. You know why he yells? Because he hasn't been fed for a spell. What's your name?'

'Carl Travis.' As the rangeman said this he looked long and hard at the sheriff. 'Why ain't he been fed?'

'The town council can't afford it.'

This time the rangeman's steady look

showed a dawning suspicion. 'You're tellin' me we talk or I don't get fed?'

'Somethin' like that.'

'What do you want to know? First off, I'll tell you I hired on as a summer rider. I do what Mister Moran says. That's what we all do.'

'If he says go lynch a squatter you do it?'

The man who said his name was Carl Travis shifted his cud from one cheek to the other one before answering. 'You better talk to Mister Moran. Like I said, he tells us to go hunt up first-calf heifers an' that's what we do.'

'You're pretty good at pullin' calves, are you?'

'I've done my share.'

The sheriff leaned back off his desk. 'A man who can pull calves ought to be handy at takin' the slack out of hang ropes, wouldn't you say?'

'I never pulled on no hang rope, an' that's the gospel truth!'

'Who did? Carl, Mister Moran can't

help you. Lie to me an' sure as we're sittin' here . . . '

'I didn't lie to you!'

'Good, because I hate liars. Carl . . . '

'I'm not goin' to tell you any more!'

The sheriff leaned forward again, studied the rangeman and slowly said, 'Partner, you don't have no fat to fall back on.' Corning arose, reached for the key ring and jerked his head.

The rangeman did not move.

'Get up you son of a bitch or I'll yank you up!'

The man named Travis did not move except to dart his tongue out and around his lips. 'I know who hung that squatter.'

Corning held the key ring in his hand as he said, 'Who?'

'A Lefler rider named Hewlett.'

Corning sat back down. 'You saw him do it?'

'Me'n the others rode out that night to scare squatters. We rode around their shacks shootin' into the houses. We met some Lefler riders. The redheaded one told us he jumped out his horse an' his squatter's neck stretched a foot.'

The sheriff said nothing for a moment or two then arose again and jerked his head. 'That redhead will be in the cell next to yours. Get up!'

The rangeman arose. He also said, 'They'll kill me.'

Corning shook his head. 'They'll never know what you told me. Carl, a word of advice, when you get loose go draw your wages, hit the trail an' don't stop ridin' until you're two hunnert miles away. Let's go.'

'You'll turn me loose?'

'Yes, but not yet awhile. *Move!*'

The sheriff was braced for what would happen when he appeared in the cell room and it happened. His redheaded prisoner ignored the Moran rider, grabbed the steel straps in the front of his cell and demanded to be fed. When Corning told him to drink water, Hewlett cursed him and would have shaken the steel he was clinging to if he could have.

The sheriff turned his back, unlocked an empty cell opposite Hewlett's cage, jerked his head and after Travis walked past he locked the door, ignored Hewlett's yelling and returned to his office. He had no illusions: when Peter Moran returned and found his bunkhouse empty he would explode. Corning expected him to arrive in town loaded for bear, and he waited. A cowman did appear but late in the afternoon while Rufe Kelly and the sheriff were having coffee.

It wasn't the fierce-tempered cowman from the south-east, it was Jonas Lefler and he had ridden to town alone. When he entered the jailhouse office, he nodded to both the lawmen, said, 'It's goin' to be a good season.' When this statement elicited no response he also said, 'If it rains,' and this time the sheriff spoke.

'Jonas, get to the point.'

The older man thumbed back his hat and shoved out his legs and then smiled at Corning. 'A1, we been friends a long time. We haven't always seen eye to eye but we got along.'

The sheriff gazed steadily at the cowman. Lefler called him Al only rarely, and he had never before spoken quietly.

Corning took the bull by the horns. 'We got Pete Moran's riders locked up an' we got your redheaded rider; an' one other thing, we know what happened at that squatter's place. Red Hewlett jumped out his horse an' broke the squatter's neck.

'Jonas, I don't need much more to write up charges for the circuit rider.'

The older man listened with his squinty-eyed look, hitched to get more comfortable in his chair and spoke in the same quiet, conciliatory voice when he said, 'That ain't the real issue is it?'

Corning said, 'Go on.'

'Yestiddy afternoon a pair of squatters shot at one of my riders. They're lousy shots, didn't hit 'em but you can't expect me to take kindly to somethin' like that, can you?'

Sheriff Corning leaned on his desk with clasped hands. 'I warned you, Jonas.'

'That's what I come to town about, Al. I don't know what your law books say, but all my life we've figured folks got a right to defend themselves.'

Corning nodded. 'Tell that to the squatters. I warned you they would hit back.'

'Al, those boys of mine was out lookin' for sore-footed cows. They was on open-range country.'

Rufe Kelly spoke sarcastically. 'Did they expect to find sore-footed cows close to a squatter's yard?'

Lefler ignored the deputy, didn't even look at him when he spoke. He looked at Sheriff Corning. 'What I come to town about, Al, is to tell you that when it gets around a couple of my riders been shot at by squatters, every rancher in the countryside'll be real upset.

'You said you wanted to prevent a range war. That's why I'm settin' here. Now's your chance. You get them squatters settled down; the next time they shoot at a rangeman the sky's goin' to fall on them. You think they got rights an' we think the cowmen got rights.'

The sheriff gambled on his next remark. 'How did the meeting go, Jonas?'

'What meeting?'

'The one yestiddy at your place with the cowmen.'

Lefler crossed his legs at the ankles before speaking again. 'It went well enough. There was hotheads wanted to hit the squatters hard, burn 'em out.' Lefler raised his slitted eyes. 'I talked 'em out of it.'

Rufe said, 'Sure you did,' and, as before, Lefler ignored the deputy to concentrate on the sheriff.

'A1, it's goin' to be touch an' go. You tell them sodbusters any more shootin' at rangemen an' we'll run every blessed one of 'em out of the country.'

Lefler returned to solemnly studying the toes of his scuffed boots. 'I hired a fee lawyer, Al. He wants to talk to you.'

'I'll be around, Jonas.'

'I'd rather settle this amongst us.' Lefler looked up again. 'We don't want no range war any more'n you do.'

Rufe spoke again. 'Tell that to the kids an' widows of the squatters you hanged.'

This time the old man turned on the deputy. 'You got a bad mouth, Deputy.'

Rufe did not interrupt again; he looked stonily at the sheriff as though the cowman did not exist.

Lefler shoved up to his feet, said, 'I hoped when we talked things could be worked out.'

The sheriff also stood up. 'They can; stay away from the squatters.'

Lefler was at the door with his hand on the latch when he said, 'Pete Moran's not goin' to like you skulkin' into his yard when he was gone and arrestin' his riders. Al, you're makin' it hard for me to keep the ranchers settled.'

After Lefler had departed, Corning sat back down at his desk in thought. Eventually he said, 'I've known that old goat since I came to this country, an' this was the first time I ever heard him makin' sense.'

Rufe went to the *olla*, drank and returned to his seat. 'He's a two-faced old son of a bitch an' you know it.'

Sheriff Corning leaned back looking at the far wall. 'Rufe, if he meant what he said . . .'

'He soft-talked you, Sheriff. A tiger don't change his spots.'

'Maybe. Maybe not, but all the same we'd better circulate among the squatters an' tell 'em not to shoot at rangemen. It'll only make matters worse.'

Rufe scratched inside his shirt, was still doing that when Horace King came in, closed the door at his back and said,

'Moran just rode in. He's down at the livery barn.'

The sheriff was not surprised; he'd expected him earlier.

The rawboned deputy said something else. 'Him an' Jonas Lefler met over near the café. They was talkin' as they went inside. Wasn't Lefler just in here?'

Corning nodded and Rufe Kelly shifted on his bench without speaking except to dourly say, 'Coincidence, Sheriff?'

Horace King waited for the sheriff's reaction. It was a long wait. 'Moran can have his riders when I'm through talkin' to them,' he said, and the rawboned lawman remained in front of the door.

'He's a nasty man, Sheriff. Maybe me'n Rufe ought to hang around.'

Corning shrugged. 'If you wish.'

Horace went to the same bench Rufe Kelly was occupying. There was a long silence before Rufe spoke. 'If the cowmen met at Lefler's place yesterday no matter what Jonas told you, I'd say it was like a gatherin' of the clans. Al, there's trouble comin' as sure as I'm settin' here. Goin' out yonder to tell the squatters not to shoot at rangemen is goin' to make the squatters think you're on the side of the ranchers.'

Although Al Corning was a patient and tolerant man, like all men of his kind, he had a limit.

He looked straight at Rufe. 'No matter what we do, boys, each side is goin' to figure we're against 'em. I'm gettin' tired of this whole damned mess. No more shootin' at rangemen an' no more lynchin' by cowmen!'

6

Palavering

When large Pete Moran burst into the jailhouse office his eyes were shooting sparks. He ignored the deputies, stood wide-legged with clenched fists in front of the seated sheriff and said, 'Didn't have the guts to raid my yard when I was there, did you! I'll give you five minutes to turn my riders loose. *Five gawdamned minutes, you old son of a bitch!*'

For several seconds before the sheriff spoke it was quiet enough in the office to hear a pin drop.

'We didn't know you wasn't home. I figured you would be. Pete, aidin' an' abettin' a fugitive is against the law. For two bits I'd put you in the cell with your riders.'

'Aidin' an' abettin' ... what the

hell are you talkin' about? I didn't aid nor . . . '

'Red Hewlett. I got him locked up. He was out there with his runnin' horse.'

'What about him? He don't work for me.'

'We know who he works for an' we know he killed a squatter named Snelling. Pete . . . '

'I don't know Red Hewlett. If he was on my place he must've come after I left.'

Sheriff Corning made a sardonic small smile. 'You was there when he arrived.'

'Prove it, you old . . . '

'You cuss me out once more, Pete, an' you'll end up in Doc's hospital room. How do I know? One of your riders told me you was there.'

The large, bullying man loosened and did not speak again for some seconds, and when he did speak his voice was once more modulated. He passed over the sheriff's threat. 'If he was there before I left he must have been put up by my riders.'

Sheriff Corning shook his head. 'You're goin' to tell me you brought a horse into the barn to be rigged out an' didn't see a sweaty horse in a stall? Pete, you can have your riders when I'm through with 'em. You want some advice? Pay 'em off an' next time hire tougher men. You care for a cup of coffee?'

Moran spun and yanked open the roadway door, slammed it after himself and Horace King said, 'Lefler'll be waitin' at the Palace,' and the sheriff nodded.

'Let's ride, boys. Them squatters is scattered over a considerable distance.'

They left with the sheriff, who locked the door after them and met the preacher. Sitwell said, 'No one tried to bust your prisoner out, but I can tell you if you don't feed that man he's going to get skinny as a snake.'

Sheriff Corning ignored the advice,

thanked the preacher for minding the jailhouse and led off in the direction of the livery barn.

The day was more than half spent, something Rufe Kelly noticed but did not comment about; he was uncomfortable about riding after nightfall among squatters' shacks. Even wearing badges, nightriders could not expect to be welcome.

If this idea occurred to the sheriff he kept it to himself. The first place they came to was no more than a mile and a half from the outskirts of town and as they approached a man and a boy stood in a ramshackle barn doorway watching. The man handed a milk bucket to the boy, spoke briefly with him and sent him to the house.

The settler recognized two of the horsemen, the sheriff and Rufe Kelly, he had seen them many times in Laramie when he went for supplies.

His old coat was ragged at the neck and cuffs. He was no more than average height and could have been anywhere between thirty-five and forty-five. His name was Jake Holzer.

As the riders got closer he went to a wall bench outside the ramshackle barn and sat down to wait. When Sheriff Corning raised a hand the squatter nodded his head without returning the salute.

There was no tie rack for a good reason, Jake Holzer owned a milk cow but no horses.

The sheriff swung down and introduced himself. The weathered man on the bench nodded again without speaking. Once his gaze moved. That was when Rufe and Horace dismounted.

Corning said, 'You'll be . . . ?'

'Jake Holzer, Sheriff.'

'Mister Holzer, some settlers shot at a pair of rangemen awhile back.'

Holzer nodded.

'It can't happen again,' the sheriff said.

Jake Holzer was expressionless and obviously wary. 'Sheriff, there's been four settlers lynched by night-ridin' rangemen. We figure that's enough.'

Corning's reply was quietly given. 'It's my job to find the nightriders, not the settlers' job.'

Holzer's reply was dry. 'It don't seem to us you're very good at catchin' them, Sheriff. Nothing personal meant. Four dead settlers is enough.'

Corning trailed his reins through both hands drawing them even. 'I got the one that killed Mister Snelling locked up.'

'That might settle up for one: how about the other three?'

'We'll get them too,' the sheriff said. 'If you folks shoot at any more rangemen you'll start a range war, an' that's what I'm tryin' to prevent.'

'How, Sheriff? They'll come back. Folks they can't lynch they'll burn out. Do you know a cowman named Lefler?'

'Yes, I know him.'

'When those lynchers killed Snelling one of 'em beat his wife. She's seen that man in town. His name is Rod

Kellogg. He rides for Mister Lefler. Sheriff, we're waitin' for him to come to town again. We don't take kindly to beating women.'

Corning turned toward his deputies. 'You know a rider named Kellogg?' he asked, and Horace King nodded.

Corning faced the man on the bench again. 'Leave Kellogg to us.'

'Can't do that, Sheriff. I got a wife and boy, the others got women and kids too.' Holzer arose facing the lawmen. 'If any more rangemen come around like those two that got shot at, yelling that our women are whores and our children are bastards, they're going to get shot.'

Al Corning returned the settler's look with one just as obdurate. 'Don't do it, Mister Holzer. Pass the word, if they come close enough to cuss you, let me know.'

Holzer was a square-jawed, pale-eyed individual with work-swollen hands. He said, 'You prove to us you don't belong to the cowmen an' maybe we'll listen.

But take my word for it, we've had enough. We won't start a range war; the cowmen have already started it. Sheriff, all of us don't miss when we shoot.'

Holzer left the lawmen standing there and walked toward his house. Rufe said, 'If they're all like that . . . '

Horace King spoke differently. 'Lookin' at it from where they stand he's right. Several lynchings an' the law's done nothing. Sheriff, let's head back. This one will tell the others what you said, an' besides, I don't like goin' right up on to these folks at night.'

It was sound advice but the sheriff did not take it. As they left the Holzer yard the sheriff rode northeasterly. The deputies looked at each other and followed in silence.

The next squatter house had a light showing. There was also a pocket-sized dog that not only barked but ran at the riders, stopped stiff-legged with its hackles up.

This time there was a good log barn

and a log house with a tie rack out front. There was a peeled pole corral about six feet high and perfectly sound, the kind mustangers erected.

The little dog ran in, nipped Horace above the ankle and darted out of reach. Horace refused to look down. The small teeth had little more than penetrated the cloth and did not even scratch the leather beyond.

When a door was opened light spilled out. The emerging woman was poised to scold the little dog when she saw the three men approaching the house. She gasped, jumped back inside and slammed the *tranca* from the inside, effectively barring the door.

Sheriff Corning knocked on the door. When there was no response he knocked again and called out who he was. When there was no response this time he said, 'We just came from the Holzer place. We want to talk to you about the lynchings.'

After a long moment, a man cracked the door holding a cocked six-gun at belly-height. There was enough light to reflect off the badges but he did not open the door. He said, 'What do you want?'

'We want to talk to you about the lynchings an' a couple of rangemen gettin' shot at.'

The answer he got was not encouraging. 'Leave your guns outside.'

Three six-guns were put on the hardpan earth. The man with the cocked pistol opened the door wider, peered intently at the faces lighted from inside, opened the door wider and jerked his head.

The log house was a mansion compared to other settler houses. It had a parlour, a kitchen and at least two other rooms at the rear of the house.

There was a fire brightly burning on a stone hearth and the smell of cooking was strong.

Behind the man was a greying woman holding a shotgun in both hands. She said, 'Go over them, Oliver,' and the man, acting embarrassed, felt each lawman for hide-out weapons, stepped back and pointed to chairs. Corning led the way; Horace watched the shotgun. The squatter said, 'About the lynchings . . . I only know what I saw when they'd been cut down. I don't know who they were, it was dark and I was home when they rode past yelling threats.'

The sheriff was also watching the square-jawed woman with the scattergun. He addressed her. 'Ma'am, we're here to talk is all.' She did not lower the shotgun. The sheriff returned his attention to the man. 'I don't recollect meeting you.'

'Name's Moses Huddlestone. They call me Moe. This is my wife Anita.'

The sheriff nodded in both their directions. The woman neither moved nor lowered the shotgun. 'Mister Huddlestone, a day or so back some settlers shot at a couple of rangemen. What I'm tryin' to do is prevent a range war. It would help if you'd pass the word not to do that again.'

Before the man could speak, his wife said, 'Did you tell the cowmen to leave us alone? We got deeds to our land. We got as much right to be here as they have. How many of us do you think have got to be murdered before we fight back?'

Sheriff Corning shifted his attention to the square-jawed woman and said about what he'd told Jake Holzer. 'We have the lyncher in jail who killed the feller named Snelling. Ma'am, I'm tryin' to stop a range war before it . . .'

'By favouring the stockmen, Sheriff? Two range riders yelling insults don't matter. You and the ranchers want a war, we'll give you one. If we got to we'll send to the soldiers for help. Tell that to the cowmen you protect!'

If it had been a man . . . but it wasn't. Still, Corning's face reddened and his effort to keep his voice moderate wasn't quite successful.

'Ma'am, I don't protect the cowmen. I just said we have the rangeman who

111

killed Snelling locked up. He'll be tried for murder.'

'You have one lyncher. Do you know how many of us have been lynched?'

'Ma'am, damnit, they protect their own. We're doin' everythin' we can.'

'Do you know who hit Missus Snelling in the face with his fist?'

'Yes, ma'am. An' we'll get him. What I'm askin' is for no more shootin' at rangemen. If you kill one I can't stop what'll happen. They outnumber you folks three or four to one.'

The man said, 'Anita, put the gun down,' and to the sheriff's surprise she obeyed. He would have bet new money the woman wore the pants and he would have lost the wager.

Her husband addressed the sheriff. 'All right there won't be any more shooting at rangemen. Do you need help? We have three settlers who were soldiers and one who was a lawman in Texas.'

Sheriff Corning arose, readjusted his

hat and shook his head. The last thing he needed was four gun-handy squatters to help him. If he was just seen in their company . . . He said, 'I'm obliged, Mister Huddlestone. If the time comes I'll send you word; right now I'm walkin' on the edge of a knife.' Corning nodded to the square-jawed woman. 'Ma'am.'

Horace held the door open and out of nowhere the feisty little dog lunged, grabbed his britches at the ankle and hung on. Horace shook his leg. The dog growled and held on. The settler came to the door and called the dog by name. He might as well have peed in the ocean with the expectation of raising the tide.

Horace leaned, got the little dog by the neck and pulled until it let go. Horace turned and handed the dog to Huddlestone who apologized and Horace grinned. 'Any time you want to get rid of her . . . '

'It's a 'him',' the woman said over her husband's shoulder, and took the little dog from her husband.

On the way to the horses Rufe spoke for the first time. 'Horace, it's amazin' to me how animals like you.'

They left the yard at a walk, and this time the sheriff reined in the direction of town. As they were entering from up-country he said, 'Either of you want to bet that woman was one of 'em as shot at Lefler's riders.'

Horace answered immediately. 'One silver dollar, Sheriff. If she'd been one of 'em as shot she'd have hit.'

The eatery was dark when they got back as were most of the business establishments. Only the Palace glowed with light. They rode as far as the livery barn, left their animals to be cared for and went to the jailhouse which was deathly quiet.

The sheriff would have made a fire in the stove but his deputies told him good night and left. He went up to the Palace which had only a few customers, leaned tiredly on the bar and nodded to Mark Turner. The barman, who brought a bottle and a jolt glass, waited until the sheriff had downed one drink then leaned and spoke in a lowered voice.

'I don't know what you told Pete Moran but when he come in earlier he was mad enough to chew nails and spit rust. I heard him unload on Jonas Lefler. He said if Jonas hadn't called a meeting he'd've been home when you come skulkin' around. Al, he was mad as I've ever seen him.'

As the sheriff refilled the little glass he asked if Turner had heard what Lefler had said and the barman wagged his head. 'He spoke real low. I sidled close to reach for a back-bar bottle but all I heard Jonas say was, 'Be patient. We'll break that son of a bitch to lead'.'

Up at the north end of the bar, Arthur Fleming struck the bartop twice for service and Turner left the sheriff to down his second jolt, which he did, and considered the painting above the back-bar of a naked woman reclining on a sofa trailing a veil over her private parts.

It was getting late, gradually all but one or two saloon regulars departed. Turner got his long-handled snuffing pole to go around and douse the lamps when Doctor Loomis came in, wild-eyed and rumpled. He ignored everything and everybody to go toward the sheriff as he said, 'Come with me,' and turned toward the doors. Corning hesitated, until the doctor jerked his head and spoke louder. *'Come with me. Now!'*

The night was turning chilly, there were few lights. Somewhere southward a horsing mare squealed, which roused a dog. It barked briefly as Corning followed the physician down through an overgrown weed parcel of vacant land in the direction of the west-side alley. It was so dark the sheriff could not avoid all the broken bottles and out-of-round buggy wheels hidden by weeds.

When he reached the alley, Les

Loomis was impatiently waiting. The sheriff paused to get rid of nettles, looked up and down the empty alley and walked over where the doctor was standing in the middle of the alley behind the jailhouse. Across the alley where a property owner had erected a wooden fence to protect some flowers and a vegetable patch, there was a large old tree whose spread was almost wide enough to shade the entire yard.

Hanging from a low limb was a man whose ankles had been bound and whose arms had been tied behind his back.

The sheriff stood as though he could not move, which he couldn't until the physician picked up a long discarded tree branch which reached well past the fence, and gently poked the dead man until he turned, and Sheriff Corning spun to go toward the rear of his jailhouse and test the door. It was locked.

He went back where the physician had tossed the long stick aside and said, 'How did you find him?'

'On my way back from treating old lady Backus for her bronchitis and took the alley short cut. Do you recognize him?'

The sheriff nodded without speaking. There wasn't enough night-light to limn the contorted face very well, but the light was adequate to show red hair.

7

Range Warclouds Building Up

The rear jailhouse door was barred from the inside by a stout *tranca* which fitted into a hanger on the left side.

Corning and Doc Loomis went around front. That door had a broken hasp and opened with only a slight push.

The physician said, 'I'll help you cut him down,' and the sheriff's reply was short. 'He can hang there. I got somethin' else to do.'

The physician accompanied the sheriff back to his office then departed.

Corning went into his cell room expecting the cells to be empty, and they were. Back in the office he studied the roadway door. It had been jimmied with a crowbar, which meant there had been noise. He considered rousting up his deputies, instead he went out back, crossed the alley, entered the yonder yard, cut the hang rope where it had been looped twice around the trunk and stepped aside as the dead man fell.

He cut the bindings loose, pocketed them, leaned and strained. The corpse was like lead. He returned to his office, put Red Hewlett flat out facing up and did something he rarely did, went to the table, rummaged for a depleted sack of Bull Durham and rolled himself a cigarette. That it didn't taste good to a tobacco chewer was not noticed. He sat at his table gazing at the dead man.

There could be several reasons why someone had taken Hewlett across the alley and hanged him. Right at this time Corning saw no irony that the lyncher had himself been lynched.

He muttered to himself, 'Jonas, you old son of a bitch.'

He could have gone to his room at the hotel but if he had he wouldn't have slept, so he rocked back, hoisted his booted feet to the table top and listened to the silence of a town that was sleeping without a qualm.

He was still sitting like that and had smoked three more quirlys when the sun arrived. Its light made the dead man's face look contorted. He'd heard it said that dead people's facial expressions were usually peaceful and serene. Not this time. Whether it was his effort to suck air or something else, Red Hewlett's features were twisted into an almost unrecognizable grimace.

The sheriff got an old army blanket from one of the cells to cover the corpse with and was finishing this chore when Horace King walked in accompanied by the coarse-featured 'breed deputy named Mike Sears who rarely spoke.

They stopped in their tracks. The sheriff leaned to uncover the face. The 'breed was like a statue, mute and surprised more than shocked but Horace went closer to look, then turned away, slumped on a bench and said,

'Squatters, Sheriff?'

'I don't think so. The other prisoners was let loose. The squatters wouldn't do that, they'd hang the lot of 'em.'

Rufe Kelly arrived, wiping his mouth with a red bandanna. He did as the others had done, he stopped stone-still staring. But he recovered more quickly. 'Them Moran men gone?' he asked, and when the sheriff nodded Rufe said the rest of it. 'Cowmen sure as hell.'

Horace took that up. 'Why, he was one of their own?'

'That's why, Horace. He likely knew more about lynchin' than the others. Bein' dead he can't talk.'

The sheriff said, 'I'd take it kindly if you boys'd carry him up the alley to Doc's shed. When you get back I think we'd better go lyncher-hunting.'

The phlegmatic 'breed slung Hewlett over a shoulder and nodded for Horace to open the back door.

Rufe remained on his bench watching the sheriff who sat at his table considering the place where the dead man had been lying. 'Jonas'll know how they did it, Rufe.'

Kelly looked sour when he replied, 'He'll be expectin' us. Him an' his fee lawyer from Cheyenne.'

Corning rocked back off the table. 'You had breakfast?' he asked.

Rufe arose and went to the door. The sheriff followed. The caféman had fired up his stove an hour earlier. His counter was partly full when the lawmen arrived. As they found places at the counter, a rangeman named Ewing called to them. 'How's the squatter business?' It was the wrong variety of sarcasm and it was also the wrong time to use it.

Rufe started to arise. The sheriff put a hand on Rufe's arm. 'Leave it be,' he said. Rufe sat back down but the look he put on the rangeman spoke volumes.

Arthur Fleming elbowed the range-man. He and the others went back to their meal, not another word was said until the lawmen left, then the storekeeper glared at the rangeman. 'You danged idiot. He's been on edge for weeks. Your mama should've taught you there's a time to talk an' a time not to.'

Horace and the 'breed were in the office when the sheriff and Rufe Kelly returned. They waited.

The sheriff went into his cell room to briefly examine the doors, something he couldn't have done in the dark. Each cell had been unlocked, the locks were on the floor. When he returned to the office, tugged loose the gun-rack chain and selected a carbine the others followed his example.

There was one deputy missing and when Horace volunteered to find him, Al Corning shook his head.

At the livery barn the proprietor saw them enter carrying booted saddle guns and wordlessly hurried to bring up horses and help in the rigging out.

Sheriff Corning led off up the west-side alley to minimize local interest. As

124

he rode past the hang tree he told his companions that was where he had cut Hewlett down. He asked Horace what Doc had said and the rawboned man answered dryly, 'He said Hewlett'd been hangin' there long enough to get stiff an' to turn loose.'

'Anythin' else?'

'He stripped him an' told us Hewlett had put up one hell of a fight. He said whoever we go after ought to have skinned knuckles at the least.'

They angled to meet the north-south coach road, remained on it until the sheriff rode over the berm heading north-east. There was no need for questions. If the youngest deputy had been along there probably would have been some but he was back in town.

Rufe had his customary expression of brooding displeasure. The odds were three to maybe six. Counting Jonas, seven.

They had big trees in sight when an angling horseman coming from the direction of town in a flat-out run began hallowing from some distance back.

They reined up to wait. Horace said, 'Holzer, the feller we talked to yestiddy.'

Corning said, 'Get down. A horse's back isn't a chair.'

They were standing with their animals when the squatter slackened the last hundred or so yards. He was wearing the same unwashed old farmer's jacket and britches he'd been wearing when the lawmen last saw him.

He ignored the deputies, rode directly up to the sheriff, who got a bad feeling before the settler spoke in a harsh and bitter voice.

'They burnt the Snelling place to the ground, run off Wayne Dunning's animals and set his house afire too, but they got it put out before it caught real good.'

Holzer leaned on his saddlehorn and looked steadily at the sheriff. 'Now we're goin' after 'em, an' Mister Corning, we got men who know how to do it.' Holzer paused. 'You on your way to the Lefler place, are you? You can tell Mister Lefler before we're finished he's goin' to wish he never started it.' Holzer paused before speaking again. 'Unless you're goin' to visit him, an' the two of you can have a drink together.'

Holzer whirled his horse and rode north-westerly, this time in an easy lope.

The sheriff watched Holzer for a moment before resuming his ride in the direction of the Lefler yard. Horace said, 'He thinks you are hand in glove with the stockmen.'

Al Corning did not comment until they were nearing the yard where several men doing chores saw them and stood waiting. 'I think Mister Holzer's goin' to keep his word. Gents, I don't think we can prevent a range war.'

Jonas Lefler appeared on his porch as he'd done before with two of his riders behind him and slightly to one side.

The sheriff tied up and a slouching

rangeman in the barn opening watched as his deputies did the same. He was chewing a stalk of grass, wearing a smug expression. As the lawmen started to cross toward the main house the slouching man straightened up and Rufe Kelly turned back, walked up to the rangeman, yanked the chewed stalk away and poked a thick finger against the rangeman's chest as he said, 'Don't go near the horses. You understand, you unwashed son of a bitch. Don't go near 'em!'

The rangeman neither moved nor spoke. He knew the look in the deputy's eyes.

At the porch, Jonas offered coffee and smiled. The sheriff ignored the offer, did not climb the steps to the porch and said, 'Did you get much sleep last night, Jonas?'

The older man answered, 'I do every night. Why shouldn't I?'

'I cut your rider down, the one with red hair.' Sheriff Corning paused before telling an outright lie with no twinge of conscience. 'You know an old woman named Backus in town, Jonas?'

'Not that I recollect. Why?'

'Because she saw the hanging.'

One of the riders behind Lefler shot a quick look at his employer and back to the lawmen. Jonas hung fire before replying. 'Sheriff, I got no idea what you're talkin' about.'

'You told Pete Moran not to worry, you had somethin' in mind.'

'I don't recollect sayin' anythin' like that.'

Corning lightly scratched the tip of his nose with his left hand during a silent interlude before speaking again.

But before the sheriff could speak, a tall man wearing city clothes — a coat and britches that matched and a necktie — came out on to the porch. He said, 'Sheriff, my name is Norman Ballester, I represent Mister Lefler as his lawyer.'

Jonas got a slight quirked-up smug smile as he addressed Corning again, 'Mind what you say, Sheriff.'

The Cheyenne lawyer seemed annoyed at that and spoke directly to the sheriff. 'Your name is Corning? Mister Corning, I think I should warn you that unless you can prove anything against Mister Lefler you'd better not threaten him.'

Rufe snorted. 'The proof, Mister Lawyer, was hanged last night across the alley from the jailhouse.'

Ballester considered Rufe briefly before returning his steady gaze to Sheriff Corning. If what Rufe had said meant anything to Ballester it didn't show. 'Sheriff, if you came out here to make trouble be warned; I can get a writ and lock you up in your own jailhouse.'

That was too much for Horace King. He abruptly turned on his heel, crossed to the tie rack, went behind the horses to the smug rangeman who was chewing a grass stalk again, and hit the man so hard in the soft parts the rangeman dropped to his knees, lost his grass stalk and covered his middle with both hands.

Horace leaned, flung the injured rider's six-gun as far as he could throw it, unlooped the reins and led the horses to the front of the porch. Rufe and the sheriff took their reins. Rufe swung up but the sheriff had one more thing to say. 'About those squatters that got burntout last night, Jonas; next time we meet you bring along your greenhorn lawyer and both of you better be armed.'

None of the men on the porch moved nor spoke as the sheriff, Rufe and Horace swung astride, turned and rode without haste out of the yard.

As they breasted the low landswell from which the Lefler yard was visible, Sheriff Corning said, 'Well, that's it, boys. We did our best to prevent it . . . that old, squinty-eyed bastard back yonder couldn't let it alone. Those squatters taken all they figure they have to an' I'll tell you, I don't blame 'em.'

Horace shook his head when Rufe offered the makings. Like the sheriff, he was a chewing man. In his private opinion, cigarettes were for dance-hall girls and anyone else who squatted to pee.

When they got back to the jailhouse, Doc Loomis was sitting out front on a bench with initials carved over most of it.

He arose, followed the lawman inside and addressed the sheriff. 'Did you see any skinned knuckles?'

Corning shook his head. 'Didn't get a chance to look for 'em. Why?'

'Because a few minutes ago, Mark came up to my place breathing like he'd run a race. There were two rangemen at his saloon, both with bruised hands and one with a lump on his jaw.'

The sheriff had a question. 'Anythin' worthwhile on the corpse, Doc?'

'Like I told your lads, he put up one hell of a fight. When I went over him after they left — he had two broken fingers on his right hand and he was gagged with someone's red bandanna before they strung him up.'

132

Corning nodded. He had the red bandanna. He also had Hewlett's sidearm and a few personal things from his pockets. 'Doc, you can certify him dead in your ledger book an' if you'd do me a favour you can get the carpenter to make him a box and see to his burial.'

Doctor Loomis studied Corning wearing a faint scowl. 'Did you look around by the tree?'

'I figure to do that now. Did you?'

'Just out of curiosity. There are three boot tracks, all different sizes and one of 'em wore his spurs out a notch so they'd make drag marks. Sheriff, that means stockmen to me.'

Corning agreed and after the physician had departed he sank down at his table facing three expressionless men on a bench across the room. Horace said, 'Jonas is goin' to be hard to handle with that fee lawyer actin' like his shadow.'

The sheriff nodded. 'For a fact. You boys get somethin' to eat. I'll be up at the Palace.'

133

The saloon was beginning to have customers. Before the day was over it would have twice as many. Single men visited bars any time they felt like it. With married men it was different, sometimes it was down-right difficult.

Mark Turner brought a bottle and a glass, set them in front of the sheriff and would have departed to serve a noisy townsman at the lower end of the bar until the sheriff asked him a question.

'Mark, yestiddy afternoon or maybe later when Jonas an' Pete Moran was here — was there any riders with 'em?'

Turner growled at the insistent customer at the lower end of the bar to be patient before he answered. 'Jonas had his range boss an' two riders. Pete Moran was by himself.'

The impatient customer at the lower end of the bar began drumming on the bartop. Mark Turner went scowlingly to serve him. When he returned, the sheriff was gone and a tall, weathered

134

man was in his place. The weathered man put a coin on the bar and reached for the bottle and glass the sheriff had left. Mark Turner scooped up the coin, went up the bar to deposit it in his cash drawer as a townsman hissed at him. When the barman turned, the townsman jerked his head sideways and whispered, 'Squatter!'

Turner looked southward where the weathered man was refilling the little glass. After so many years tending bar, a man got so he set them up without heeding whom he served.

The townsman was right, the weathered man wore an ancient coat that had been patched and rumpled, stained trousers. His hat had a narrow brim.

Mark leaned to look lower, saw the bulge of a holstered sidearm and lace shoes caked with mud.

The settler caught Mark studying him and shoved away both the bottle and the glass as he returned Turner's stare and quietly spoke. 'You got a law no settlers allowed in here, friend?'

Turner reddened as he straightened back. 'No sir. Anyone with two bits is welcome.'

The settler then said, 'Do you ever give a free drink to cowmen, friend?'

Turner was having a bad premonition. 'I do, an' to them as aren't cowmen. Would you like one on the house?'

The settler straightened back off the counter when he nodded and swept back the right side of his dirty old jacket.

Mark went down the bar, refilled the glass and made a forced smile. 'On the house — friend.'

There was not a sound and no movement as the squatter downed his second jolt, then turned everyone to stone including Mark Turner when he twisted a little and shot three times. Each slug punched a candle out of its holder.

The settler nodded and walked out into the oncoming dusk.

Someone spoke in a hushed voice.

'Chris' a' mighty,' got to his feet at a card table and left. Three other customers also left but none of them made a sound.

Mark Turner leaned to look at the shattered candles. They had been in holders positioned over a poker table in a part of the room where the hissing chandeliers shed insufficient light.

An old man said, 'Damned good thing he didn't shoot higher; he'd have busted one of them fancy fixtures.'

Normalcy did not quite return but talking broke the stunned silence. A man wearing a muleskin apron with little slits on each side, who had to be a blacksmith, no one else wore an apron like that, called for another drink and as Turner set up the glass and bottle the aproned man smiled at him. 'Last time I saw shootin' like that was at a county fair in Kansas when the shooter was a woman. Ugly enough to gag a buzzard, but she could shoot rings around anyone I ever saw. Mark, do you know that squatter?'

The old man who had mentioned the chandeliers put in another two-bits' worth when he said, '*Mister* squatter, friend,' which brought forced smiles.

The barman answered the question. 'I never saw that man before in my life,' and started to remove his apron when the sheriff walked in.

He had heard the gunshots. He had also seen a raggedy-looking tall man leaving town astride a big saddle mule. They had exchanged nods.

Five voices erupted at once as the sheriff walked in. Mark Turner pointed to the shattered candles and their holders. As he explained, the other witnesses either got quiet or left.

Corning listened to the description of the shootist, remembered nodding to a raggedy-assed man riding a Missouri mule and when he got tired of exaggerations and the same stories being endlessly repeated, he went out into the night, breathed deeply and headed for the hotel.

One thing was a lead-pipe certainty:

there was one squatter worth thinking about. If nightriders made a run on the settler's place Doc Loomis was going to have more cold bodies in his embalming shed.

8

The Shootist

Rufe Kelly and Horace King were having breakfast at the café when they heard a circulating rumour. Someone had been hanged across the alley behind the jailhouse and inevitably some wag said the sheriff knew how to take care of troublemakers.

They finished eating and crossed to the jailhouse where the sheriff told them of the boot tracks and marks around the hanging tree left by someone who wore his spurs down a couple of notches. When he mentioned Hewlett's torn and battered hands, Rufe interrupted. 'That one shouldn't be hard to find,' and the sheriff agreed with a nod of his head.

He didn't want to return to the Lefler place, not yet anyway, so he suggested a ride to the Moran place and Horace scotched that. 'He's only got one man left. The others come through this morning to stock up at the emporium. They told Mister Fleming they'd quit.'

The sheriff sighed inwardly. The lynchers had been stockmen. Possibly they hadn't been Jonas's riders but for a fact, according to Mark Turner, Jonas'd had three riders with him in town and it didn't require a crystal ball to wonder if those Lefler riders hadn't been Hewlett's lynchers.

He still did not want to go out there again so soon. He asked if the deputies had heard about the rough-looking squatter shooting out candles at the Palace last night and they nodded. Rufe made a dry comment close to what the sheriff had thought last night in bed. He said, 'If the nightriders raid his place they're goin' to get a surprise.'

Horace asked which homestead the gunman owned and Corning couldn't answer. He didn't even know the squatter's name. He told Horace to go to the Palace, someone up there might have the information, and Horace left the office.

Rufe slowly and methodically built a cigarette and lighted it before saying, 'Sheriff, why would stockmen hang Hewlett?'

'Because he knew about what's been goin' on; we had him locked up, an' for all they knew we might get him to help us.'

Rufe trickled smoke. He was not convinced that would be the reason. 'From what I saw of him Hewlett wouldn't open up if his feet was stuck in a fire. All they had to do was pay him off with a bonus and send him on his way.'

Rufe made sense, except for one thing and the sheriff mentioned it. 'Jonas Lefler grew up hard. He's lived hard all his life. If he felt threatened he knew the best way to take care of it.'

When Horace returned he said, 'Mark didn't know but an old gummer drinkin' free drags did. He said the feller's name is Bertram. He didn't recollect the first name. He said Bertram lived a couple miles northwest of the Holzer place, lives by himself on a poor piece of land close to the foothills.'

The sheriff reset his hat, thanked Horace and went to the gun rack. As he was booting a carbine, Rufe said, 'Those foothills run for thirty miles east and west.'

Corning's answer was brusque. 'It's early. We got all day.'

The sheriff didn't intend to spend the day looking for the Bertram place. When he and his deputies left town he rode up the coach road a fair distance then reined off it and Rufe looked at Horace who nodded in silent agreement. They were heading in the direction of the Holzer place and got there with the sun still climbing. An erect woman with greying hair pulled severely back and bunned, stood just outside the house doorway watching.

The men were not intimidated but as they went toward the house they were braced for unpleasantness and the grim-faced woman did not disappoint them.

Before the sheriff could speak the woman said, 'If you came to see my husband, he's not here.' She raised an arm. 'You see those tall sentinel pines yonder?'

They turned and looked. Corning nodded as he turned back. The woman said, 'That's where Jake is. At the Bertram place.'

Corning turned again, fixed the huge old pines in sight, thanked the woman, got astride and left the yard. A mile out he asked if either of his companions had ever explored the foothills. Neither had. The sheriff rode until they came to a creek and swung off to drink and water their animals, and spoke while leaning across his saddle seat.

'I got a feelin' about this, boys.'

Rufe was running a sleeve across his lower face when he said, 'So have I.'

It was Horace who was rebridling his horse who said, 'All's I got is a growin' hunger.'

Neither the sheriff nor Rufe Kelly mentioned the subject again until, with the sun slightly off centre and they had those two big sentinel pines only another few miles ahead, Rufe said, 'You want to bet, Al? That's a long ride for Holzer, he'd have a reason to make it. Want to bet?'

Corning shook his head without looking around. Rufe spoke again, 'There'll be more than just Holzer up there,' and Horace looked around sharply; what his friends had been alluding to hit him like a stone but he said nothing as they continued riding, but Horace sat straighter in the saddle and tipped down his hat brim to shade alert and wary eyes.

They'd been crossing open grassland for a considerable length of time and were no more than about a mile from the towering sentinel pines which stood a good five feet above other backgounding foothill pines and firs, when a man carrying a carbine across his lap came out of an arroyo on a big pudding-footed harness animal and stepped in their path.

He didn't raise his right hand in the customary salute between mounted men, he simply blocked their trail until they were close enough, then he raised his voice a little as he said, 'Sheriff, you're a long way from town.'

Corning agreed. 'Yes sir. I'm lookin' for Jake Holzer. His woman told us he was up here at the Bertram place,' which wasn't exactly what she had said but it was close enough providing the armed man on the big horse replied the way Corning hoped he would, and he did.

'Jake's back yonder. So is Bert. You mind tellin' me what you want?'

The sheriff rested both hands atop the saddle horn as he returned the other man's gaze. 'I wouldn't mind, friend, except that I'd rather not have to say it twice.'

Before the armed man could reply several bursts of gunfire erupted. Corning squinted ahead for gunpowder smoke. There was none. He shifted slightly in the saddle and returned his attention to the man on the twelve-hundred-pound horse. 'Rifle practice, friend?'

The reply was not delayed. 'Somethin' like that . . . Sheriff, do yourself a favour, turn around and go back the way you come.'

The sheriff did in fact raise his left hand with the reins in it but he didn't turn back, he squeezed his mount and rode directly at the man with the Winchester across his lap. At the last moment he swerved, rode around the man and kept on riding.

Horace King and Rufe Kelly did the same. The sheriff had not looked at the man on the pudding-footed horse as he passed and neither did Horace, but Rufe did, and he said, 'Mister, ride along with me. I never cared for someone behind my back holdin' a gun.'

The man turned his big horse and did exactly as Rufe had asked. Rufe smiled a little. 'How long you been watchin' us, friend?'

'Since you was three, four miles along from the Holzer place.'

'You got a name, friend?'

The Winchester-man looked stonily at Rufe as he answered, 'What's your name, Deputy?'

'Rufe Kelly . . . yours?'

'Well . . . '

'That's all right, squatter. John Smith will be just fine.'

'It's Frank Bulow. What do you want to see Jake Holzer about?'

The sheriff twisted to look back as he said, 'We want to see Mister Bertram.'

The man named Bulow was probably not as old as he looked. People weathered fast when two-thirds of their days were spent outside, particularly in windy country.

He was compactly put together, had thinning hair under a battered old

148

Stetson hat and, although he had looked downright menacing where he'd intercepted the lawmen, now, riding with Rufe Kelly he looked more uncomfortable than upset.

The house up ahead was adequately backgrounded by foothill forest to be unnoticeable from a distance. There was also a log barn with an assortment of lesser log buildings.

Whoever had done the constructing had been experienced. Even the pole tie rack in front of the barn was set so well the best halter-pulling horse on earth couldn't move it.

There was no more gunfire. In fact, until a tall man in disreputable attire appeared in the barn opening from out back somewhere, with two other disreputable-appearing squatters, the lawmen saw no one.

As the sheriff tied up he nodded to the tall man and remembered him from the darkness when he'd been straddling a big mule. He took a chance. 'Mister Bertram . . . '

The rugged individual gravely inclined his head. 'Just plain Bert, Sheriff. Is there somethin' I can do for you?'

Two men came from the direction of a three-sided shoeing shed, did not make a sound as they stopped about fifteen feet behind the lawman, until one man cleared his throat and Rufe looked around.

One of the men was Jake Holzer who nodded and looked dispassionately at the sheriff's back.

Bertram had a deep, strong voice which he did not raise when he again addressed the sheriff.

'We're doing a little target practice, Sheriff. It's not against the law is it?'

Al Corning considered the tall man with the steely-blue eyes and did not answer. Instead he said, 'Mister Bertram, I expect you can make tolerable good shots of 'em. What I'm tryin' to do is prevent a fight, not brace for one.'

The tall man in his soiled old jacket

and trousers fixed the sheriff with a cold gaze. 'The settlers have suffered enough. A man shouldn't have to go to bed scairt of every sound. Or maybe get his neck stretched by some lynch-happy son of a bitch on a ranch horse.'

'That one,' Corning said, 'is dead.'

Bertram showed surprise, then disbelief. 'Is that a fact?'

'He was hung from a tree behind my jailhouse.'

'An' you figure we did it?'

'No. I figure I know who did it. Not squatters.'

'Who, Sheriff?'

Corning put that same hard look on the tall man without answering. It was the second time he'd left the impression he would not discuss it and the tall man evidently understood because he changed the subject. 'There's a few can shoot pretty well, but mostly they can't.'

'Mister Bertram, you lead them into a fight with the ranchers an' they'll not only out-number you, they'll out-shoot you. You folks have had enough casualties.'

Bertram agreed with that. 'More than enough, Sheriff. There won't be any more.'

For the first time Rufe spoke and he did not look the least bit intimidated by the armed men in front and behind. He said, 'You kill one rangeman an' they'll put out dodgers for gunfighters . . . listen to the sheriff.'

Bertram studied the shorter, muscular deputy before returning his attention to the sheriff. 'It's up to them, not us. If they strike again we're goin' after 'em. They'll think the sky fell on 'em. Sheriff, care for somethin' to eat?'

Bertram had a deep pit covered with a heat-resistant large grill. There were men tending the coals and the cooking meat. The squatters were mostly reticent but not unpleasant. A broad-faced blond man who handed out platters of cooked beef and potatoes said, 'It's not cowman beef, gents.'

No one laughed.

The coffee had been boiled so many times it could almost stand upright unaided. The lawmen ate as did the squatters each one of whom wore a sidearm with the tie-down hanging loose. Jake Holzer avoided the lawman. A woman whose face had been swollen and discoloured the last time Corning had seen it, stood apart with two other women, refusing to even look at the lawmen.

Later, Bartram accompanied the lawmen back to their horses. As they strolled he said, 'It's not just fighting back, Sheriff, which we'll do like they done, ride in fast on a dark night and lynch 'em, it's the matter of burnt-out houses and outbuildings, run-off livestock, callin' dirty names when they ride past . . . it's all those things and more.'

The sheriff stopped looking at the tall man. 'I can't undo what's been done, Mister Bertram. If you make 'em into nightriders take my word for it, they'll lose whatever they got left.'

As the lawman mounted, Bertram stood beside the sheriff's animal and said, 'We got legal title, we didn't start this, we don't expect to put up with it again. Why would someone hang that feller behind your jailhouse?'

The sheriff evened-up his reins, nodded and led the way back the way he and his deputies had come. Horace looked back and said, 'Hell!'

Rufe and the sheriff looked back. There were more than twice the number of men standing back there with the tall man than they had seen.

Rufe said, 'Hidin' out in the barn,' and sat forward.

They were roughly half-way back to town when Corning, riding slightly ahead, saw movement and halted. Four horsemen were crossing from the east to the west and were hurrying. As the lawmen watched, the horsemen went over a slight lip of land and disappeared. Rufe put it succinctly.

154

'They saw us an' made a run for it before we saw them.'

It was a fair guess because the horsemen did not appear on the far side of the arroyo. The sheriff moved out on a different heading. His course was on an angling route in the direction of the arroyo and, as he and his deputies got closer, the four horsemen burst out of the arroyo on the west side riding hard.

Horace said, 'Never catch 'em.'

The sheriff was sitting erectly watching the fleeing men when he spoke. 'I got a hunch, let's go look in the arroyo,' which is what they did and found where two men had held the horses while the other two had crept up on the easterly side of the gully and lay belly down. They were obviously the ones who went back to inform their companions the lawmen had changed course.

The sheriff stood a long time where horses had been. When Rufe and Horace came up he pointed. There were boot marks among the shod-horse tracks.

The sheriff squatted near one set of tracks, looked up the easterly slope and arose to say, 'Spur marks. One of 'em was watchin' us. Him an' his friend run back down to warn the others. See those squiggles where someone wore his spurs loose?'

Horace leaned but Rufe didn't. He looked at the sheriff. 'That one'll be the feller who beat on the woman.'

The sheriff nodded. 'Kellogg. Either of you know him?'

Neither did. The sheriff got back astride and rode out of the arroyo on the west side. There was no sign of the four riders.

They turned in the direction of town and continued on their way. The day was wearing along, both men and horses were tiring but at least the men had been fed.

When they reached the livery barn the proprietor was on a chair in the centre of the runway lighting a lamp.

He looked around, finished lowering the mantle and climbed down. Not a word was exchanged as the horses were left with the liveryman and the lawmen trooped up to the office. The sheriff nodded when Horace looked at him from the stove. Horace set about making a fire.

The sheriff sat at his table and made a guess. 'I think we interrupted somethin', them riders was pokin' around over in squatter country.'

Rufe was sceptical. 'In broad daylight?'

Corning gazed dispassionately at his deputy. 'It's not daylight now. I'd say they was scoutin'. If I was to guess further I'd say they'll raid a squatter tonight.'

Rufe made a dry remark. 'Maybe they heard shootin' up at the Bertram place.'

The sheriff didn't think so. They'd come from the east; his guess was that they'd been miles in that direction earlier in the afternoon. But he said, 'If they had in mind shootin' up the

Bertram place and hangin' someone, it just damned well could be the biggest mistake they ever made.' It was.

Wayne Dunning walked in sucking his teeth. He'd just eaten at the café. He nodded around and quietly said, 'Miz Snelling wants to go back where they come from in Missouri.' Dunning paused. 'You gents know anyone wants to buy a milk cow?'

Horace shook his head. 'She don't have any money?'

'No. My wife'n me put in three dollars.'

Sheriff Corning spoke next. 'We might need her to identify the feller who hit her.'

Dunning said, 'When, Sheriff?' And Corning had no answer except to say when the circuit-riding judge came to town, and also said, 'I can't say when that'll be. They cover a lot of territory, hold hearings in a lot of places . . . Mister Dunning, can you keep her in for awhile?'

The squatter hung fire before

answering. 'I expect we can, Sheriff, but if them lynchers know she can identify 'em . . . '

It was a good point. The two seated deputies looked steadily at the sheriff and Corning said, 'One of us can go out to your place.'

The squatter was doubtful and looked it. 'Would it do as good if she gave you a written story about what happened an' what she saw?'

The deputies continued to look at the sheriff without moving or speaking.

'It'd help,' the sheriff said, 'but if the circuit rider wants to hear it from her . . . Can you put her up for a week or two, Mister Dunning?'

The squatter yielded. 'We can. I hope the feller you put out there to watch don't need a lot of sleep. Sheriff?'

'Yes.'

'I heard there was a hanging behind your jailhouse.'

Corning nodded. 'There was.'

'We didn't have no hand in it. I can

give you my word.'

The sheriff stood up wearing a slight smile. 'I never thought you folks did.'

'Then who?'

'Go on home, Mister Dunning. I'll send a man out directly. All the same, keep a gun close an' sleep light.'

After the settler had departed, Rufe cocked an eyebrow. 'The 'breed?' he asked.

Corning nodded. 'You fellers find him, tell him what he's to do, an' tell him if any nightriders show up, shoot to kill.'

After the deputies had left, the sheriff went to stand by the little barred roadway window. He'd wanted Red Hewlett so bad he could taste it. Now he wanted the rider named Kellogg.

He had supper at the café, trudged up to his room at the hotel, shed most of his attire and went to bed. For a change, this night he slept like a dead man.

In the morning when he was out back cleaning up at the wash house his youngest deputy came hunting for him. As the sheriff entered the hotel with his razor, lye soap in hand and his towel over one shoulder, the younger man spoke breathlessly. 'There's a wagon down in front of the jailhouse. You better come.'

Sheriff Corning got a knot in the bottom of his empty stomach. He paused at his room long enough to put on his shirt, hat, and his shellbelt with the holstered Colt.

There was a small crowd across in front of Fleming's store where Rufe had growled for them to go as he and Horace King stood with the wagon and its white-faced owner.

What surprised the sheriff was that there were three dead men in the wagon. As he stared, Rufe jostled him and wordlessly pointed to the boots on one of the corpses. The spurs were loose enough to leave squiggle tracks when the man walked.

Sheriff Corning looked at the slack, coarse features and said, 'Damn! I wanted that one real bad. That's got to be the feller who beat up on the squatter woman the night Hewlett busted the squatter's neck and also one of 'em who hung Hewlett.'

Horace said, 'This here is . . . '

'I know Mister Holzer, Horace. You'n Rufe take 'em up to Doc's embalmin' shed. Tell him I'll be along later.'

The sheriff took Jake Holzer by the arm, went around the head of the harness animal and led him into the jailhouse office.

9

A Gold Coin

The stocky settler, roughly the same age as the sheriff, didn't wait to be offered a seat, he sat down on a wall bench staring through or past the sheriff.

As Corning opened his mouth to speak, Holzer said, 'I never saw anythin' like it as God is my witness. It was gettin' along, there was dusk in the yonder trees when they come in at a dead run yellin' an' shootin' . . .

'Sheriff, it was like shootin' birds roostin' in a tree. They shot up Mister Bertram's cabin as they come on. The rest of us was fixin' to ride home. Me, I was saddlin' my horse in the barn with the others . . . most of the others. It took us plumb by surprise. You'd only been gone a couple of hours . . . '

The hard-faced settler's gaze gradually settled on the sheriff's face. 'One feller was out front, reins looped, shootin' with a handgun. His horse was in a bellydown run . . . I never could've hit him, not a runnin', shootin' target like that . . . '

The sheriff said, 'Bertram, Mister Holzer?'

The settler nodded. 'We knew he'd been a Texas deputy. He told us that much. But by Gawd, I never saw the likes. He stood in front of the house wide-legged, trackin' that raider and shot him off his horse like . . . never saw the like.

'The second one, back maybe fifteen yards saw Mister Bertram, leaned to his left and fired twice.'

'Missed?'

'Both times; but Mister Bertram didn't miss. The feller went off over the rump of his horse.'

'How many were there, Mister Holzer?'

'Four. The third feller was fightin'

his horse, tryin' to rein it southward. He threw a wild shot ... Mister Bertram hit him square in the brisket. Mind you, his horse was fightin' the bit, jumpin', shyin' an' faunchin' for all he was worth. I'd bet there isn't ten men in the country that could have hit him, let alone right through the chest.'

'Mister Holzer — the fourth one?'

'He was back aways. He reined southward so hard the horse almost stumbled. He never fired a shot, he rode over that animal's neck like the Devil was after him.'

Sheriff Corning went to a box and returned with a bottle which he handed to the settler and Jake Holzer, who was not a drinking man, pulled the cork with his teeth, drank, handed back the bottle and the cork, then bent over coughing.

Sheriff Corning had more questions but his deputies returned to report they had found the 'breed deputy at the pool hall, had told him what he was to do and saw him leave town in a slow lope.

They also said Doc Loomis wanted to see him. Jack Holzer's colour had improved as he arose, nodded to the sheriff and went to look for his horse and wagon which were in the alley behind Doc Loomis's embalming shed.

As they sat, Horace spoke. 'I want to tell you, Sheriff, whoever shot those bastards could shoot the eye out of a gnat — on the fly.'

Sheriff Corning nodded. 'Bertram; that feller who was teachin' the squatters how to shoot.'

Rufe Kelly made one of his dry remarks. 'Whoever did it could've got lucky once, but not three times.' He was rolling a smoke before he said the rest of it. 'They were Lefler riders. The squatters caught three horses. The fourth one had the luck of the Irish.'

The sheriff corrected that. 'He cut off southward when he saw what happened to Kellogg an' the other one. He rode full tilt, never got off a shot an' was out of pistol range or he'd have joined the other three. It wasn't luck, it was a fast horse.'

Rufe was trickling smoke when he said, 'If those horses got a Circle L brand . . . '

Al Corning nodded. 'There's no stoppin' it now.'

The youngest deputy walked in and stopped stone still, not only did the seated men look bleak as they ignored him, but the sheriff sent him down to make sure the liveryman had hayed and grained their horses.

Mark Turner from the Palace came in still wearing his apron. He looked at the seated men and softly said, 'Then it's true. Someone shot three of Jonas Lefler's riders.'

It couldn't have been kept quiet; there had been a number of townsmen — and townswomen — watching from in front of Fleming's emporium.

No one spoke to the saloonman. In fact Horace King went to get a drink from the *olla* and kept his back to

Turner while he did that, and Rufe Kelly spit in his palm, drowned the cigarette and shoved it into the fold of his trousers at the ankle.

After the saloonman left, Horace asked the sheriff if he thought they should ride out to the Lefler place and Corning shook his head. 'He'll be along, Horace.'

It was a good surmise but the day was about half spent before Lefler appeared from the north coach road and he wasn't alone, the fee lawyer from Cheyenne was riding beside him and three rangemen brought up the rear. One of the three was sweaty and nervous. His eyes jumped from people on both sides of the road to the jailhouse up ahead. He acted like a man who would, at the slightest encouragement, ride right on through to the lower end of town, hook his horse into a run and never look back.

Lefler didn't tie up out front, he took his companions to the rack over in front of the emporium. They tied up there and Jonas leaned with both elbows on the tie pole looking steadily at the front of the jailhouse with eyes squinched nearly closed and when the necktie-wearing man beside him spoke, Jonas neither answered nor appeared to listen.

Rufe went to the window; outside, the usual noise of riders, wagons and buggies passing was lacking.

There were a few people across the road and as Rufe looked over there a tall, gaunt woman emerged from the store carrying a laden basket.

Arthur Fleming stepped to his doorway very briefly before disappearing back deeper inside.

Rufe said, 'Al,' and when the sheriff approached, Rufe also said, 'That old man's not here to talk.'

The sheriff had to lean a little to see across the road. He straightened back slowly, saw Horace watching and said, 'You boys stay in here. Cover my back if it needs covering,' and went to the door. It was much warmer in the roadway than it had been in the jailhouse. The sheriff stood for as long as was required to reset his hat then he walked slowly toward the men at the emporium's tie rack and didn't wait for Lefler to speak. He said, 'Three Circle L riders are up at Doc's embalming shed. You can have 'em any time you want 'em, otherwise we'll bury 'em in the town graveyard.'

Jonas's lips were pulled flat. His slitty gaze never deviated from his stare at the lawman and when the sheriff was beginning to think he was not going to speak, Lefler said, 'Who killed 'em? I know you was up there.'

It required no great capability to understand how Lefler had known that. His nervous rider had a glassy stare.

'You did it?' Jonas asked.

Corning shook his head. 'Jonas, they made a firing run at that settler's house. In broad daylight.'

'It was getting along to sundown,' the cowman stated.

Corning considered the older man for a moment before speaking again. 'That was a damn fool thing they did. Before it's always been after dark. Jonas, that place was full of squatters. Why didn't they scout it up first?'

The fee lawyer started to interrupt and Jonas snarled him into silence. 'Sheriff, them boys was on open range. They was lookin' for cattle. They had every right to . . .'

'You're makin' it worse, Jonas. Riders lookin' for cattle don't make a run at a place shootin' an' yellin'.'

This time the fee lawyer spoke before Lefler could. 'They'd had a few drinks. You can't arbitrarily kill people who've had a few drinks.'

The sheriff didn't even look at the lawyer. He addressed Lefler again. 'Jonas, I told you they'd strike back. You want to send a wagon for the bodies or not?'

The sheriff was turning away when Lefler said, 'You told me you wanted to prevent a war. Well, Sheriff, let me tell you straight out, now you got one on your hands!'

Corning hesitated, looking at the cowman, then walked without haste back to his jailhouse office where Rufe and Horace had been straining to hear at the little roadway window.

The sheriff said, 'All right; I did as much as I could. The old bastard said now there'd be a range war.'

Rufe Kelly was less upset than his companion. Horace moved clear of the window as he said, 'What do you want to do?' And the sheriff flung his hat on the table before replying.

'You take the stage to Cheyenne, tell whoever's in charge of the soldiers if he wants to prevent a lot of killing he'd better get down here, fast.'

Horace went outside where the Lefler men were still standing at Fleming's hitch rack and walked northward in the direction of the stage-company's corralyard. But he didn't turn in, he walked past, entered the saddle and harness shop and watched from the roadway window.

The leather man had tufts of grey hair on both sides and none above. He was working at his cutting table when Horace entered. He put aside his tools, removed his rimless glasses and said, 'Horace? You want somethin'?' and got an answer while the deputy remained in shadows watching the road.

The harness-maker got himself a cup of black java, took it back to his work table, put the cup down, sat on a chair and watched the deputy.

He was old enough to have seen just about everything at least twice. He watched the deputy in silence. When a party of horsemen passed at a walk, the harness-maker leaned to see if he could identify any of them and had no difficulty in recognizing one: Jonas Lefler.

When Horace relaxed the leather man said, 'The coffee's hot.'

Horace finally turned. 'No thanks, Henry,' he said and left the shop walking southward to the corralyard.

The harness-maker was a chewer not a smoker. He had a square box better than a foot wide around his little stove. It was filled with sand. He spat, wagged his head and went back to the cutting table.

No man lived into his sixties without learning to interpret things, and the tough, scrawny cowman the deputy had been watching rode straight up in his saddle, he was upset, and when Jonas Lefler was upset it was a good time for folks to keep their heads down.

He was right; Rufe and the sheriff knew that too. When only the two of them were in the office like a pair of grizzled dolls, Doctor Loomis walked in scowling. 'I waited,' he told the sheriff, and Corning said, 'Somethin' come up.'

The physician looked as rumpled as he usually did. He took the chair beside the roadway door, leaned far back to ease a chronic back pain, and said, 'Whoever shot those men . . . Were they on moving horses?'

The sheriff nodded. Doctor Loomis's eyes widened. 'It couldn't have been accidental. Maybe it was luck, but they were dead before they hit the ground. .44 calibre. I'd guess from a distance. Al, that's Annie Oakley kind of shooting.'

The sheriff nodded in an abstract way. Doctor Loomis's brow began to gather as he looked from the sheriff to the deputy. He arose and said, 'Does the town bury 'em?'

The sheriff finally spoke. 'Jonas Lefler'll likely come after 'em. They were his riders.'

The physician stared briefly then left the jailhouse. Rufe made a wry grin when he said, 'He'll give Jonas a healthy bill for embalmin' 'em.'

The sheriff said nothing, he was busy with some serious thoughts. He said, 'Rufe . . .'

'What.'

'Retaliation as sure as we're settin' here.'

Rufe made one of his mordant

comments. 'Sure. It's all right for them to lynch squatters, burn 'em out an' steal their livestock.' He paused before addressing a separate subject. 'How long'll it take for the army to get here — if they agree to come?'

'One day, two at the most. With the army they patrol a sizeable territory. When Horace gets up there they might have patrols out.'

Rufe shrugged. None of this was new to him. Over the years he'd had occasion to know soldiers. He arose, 'I'll fetch the mail,' he said, and left the sheriff to his unpleasant thoughts.

When Rufe entered the emporium, Arthur Fleming landed on him like a ton of bricks. 'I don't appreciate having my store used as a fort. You can tell the sheriff that. Armed deputies up front watchin' the road scairt off customers. They didn't commence to return until this morning.'

Rufe pointed to a particular pigeon-hole among many without speaking. Fleming got the mail, handed it to the deputy and, encouraged by Rufe's silence, let go with another salvo. 'If Al keeps up this vendetta with the cowmen, business in town'll drop close to zero.'

Rufe looked straight at the irate storekeeper as he said, 'What's a vendetta?' and walked out of the store.

Sheriff Corning was at the little roadway window, hands clasped behind his back. When Rufe dropped the mail on the table he said, 'Fleming didn't like having armed deputies inside his store.' When the sheriff did not answer as he sat down at the desk, Rufe added a little more. 'He said we're goin' to ruin business.'

The sheriff sifted through the mail, pushed all but two letters aside and said, 'When the soldiers get here Arthur'll have fits.'

Rufe's interest had wandered again. 'I'd like to know more about that Bertram feller. No one's born that good with a gun.'

The sheriff nodded without commenting. He put the two letters with the other mail and stood up. 'Are you hungry?' he asked, and got a direct answer, 'No, but I could use a dram of popskull.'

They went up to the Palace where it was the wrong time of day for much bar trade.

An old man sidled up close and spoke to the sheriff. 'I was comin' back from wood-gatherin' a while back an' seen riders comin' from the direction of Circle L.'

The sheriff nodded, gestured for Mark Turner to set up a drink for the old man and left the saloon walking with Rufe in the direction of Doctor Loomis's house with the sign out front and a picket fence around the front yard.

Leslie Loomis had been in his cubby-hole office when someone rattled his roadway door. He welcomed interruptions when he was doing book work and hastened to the parlour, opened the door, read the faces of his visitors and took them inside where the sheriff repeated what the old man at the Palace had told him, and Doctor Loomis accepted that information with no indication of unease.

He said, 'I've got 'em wrapped in shrouds out back with what was in their pockets in their hats.' He paused, rummaged a pocket, brought forth and held up where the lawmen could see it, a twenty-dollar gold coin.

'That's a tad more'n Jonas'll owe me but close enough.'

The sheriff took the coin, turned it over a couple of times and handed it back. At Rufe's puzzled look he said, 'He pays in silver. None of 'em pay in gold, either in silver or greenbacks. Doc, whose pocket was this in?'

'The one named Kellogg.'

Corning smiled a little. 'Do you mind if we're here when the wagon arrives for 'em?'

Doctor Loomis didn't mind. Although he shared a common dislike of Jonas

Lefler, a man in his trade was understandably discreet. He asked if the sheriff anticipated trouble and got a cryptic reply.

'Most likely not. In fact us bein' here when they arrive might aggravate things, but I doubt there'll be trouble.'

The sheriff was partly right. When the riders dismounted out front and looped their lines and Jonas, along with his city lawyer, came up the walk, the driver of the wagon kept going to the nearest intersection, then turned in as far as the alley before lining out north to stop close to the embalming shed.

When Loomis opened the door and the men on the porch saw the sheriff and his deputy in the parlour they were momentarily nonplussed.

Loomis gestured and they entered. The lawyer removed his hat, Jonas did not; he looked sulphurously past the doctor as he said, 'Do you want somethin', Sheriff?'

'No. Just thought we could lend a hand loadin' 'em.'

Jonas faced the doctor. 'Are they out back?'

'Yes.'

Lefler turned to the lawyer. 'Go tell the boys out front to go around back.'

The lawyer left without so much as a scowl and the sheriff wondered who had who in whose pocket, Jonas or the Cheyenne lawyer.

Doctor Loomis led the way from his parlour through his kitchen and beyond the back porch to the embalming shed.

When he opened the door, Rufe flinched. The smell was somewhere between formaldehyde and rotgut whiskey.

The bodies were on the floor wrapped from head to toe in cotton shrouds. Their hats were on the embalming table.

Someone rattled the door. Loomis opened it and the Circle L riders froze. They'd had no inkling there would be lawmen in the shed.

Jonas gave them an order after asking

181

if the tailgate had been lowered. One rider nodded so Jonas pointed. 'Take 'em one at a time.'

While the shrouded corpses were being carried away Doctor Loomis gestured in the direction of his table as he said, 'Those are their hats, Mister Lefler. Whatever was in their pockets I put into their hats.'

Jonas considered the hats, went to the middle one and pawed through its contents, stopped pawing and raised his eyes to the physician.

'Is that all he had, Doc?'

'Well, no. That's the one named Kellogg.' Loomis brought forth the gold coin. 'He had this too,' and when Jonas shoved out a hand palm-up the doctor smiled at him. 'This'll just about pay for laying them out, embalming them and cleaning up the bodies.' Loomis returned the gold coin to his pocket and continued to smile. Like the others he was awaiting the cowman's reaction.

There was none, Lefler said, 'I hope

I never need you, Doctor. You're kind of expensive.'

When the bodies were loaded, Lefler crossed to stand in front of the sheriff. 'Remember what I told you, Al. It's pay-back time.'

Lefler went into the alley with his men, Doctor Loomis closed the shed door and looked impassively at the sheriff. 'He didn't like me keeping the coin.' He also said, 'It went off better than I expected — you being here.'

Rufe opened the door, he was sensitive to the smell, led the way outside and back to the house.

10

Three Texans

Horace King returned late the following afternoon to tell the sheriff the soldiers would not be coming.

There was some kind of military shake-up with men being transferred. Horace had been told in bitter tones by a grizzled major that there was a move afoot to eliminate some garrisons altogether and drastically reduce the complements of other installations, and he profanely attributed this to some parsimonious sons of bitches in Congress who wanted to slash budgets.

The sheriff got another shock. Late in the afternoon of the same day Horace had returned, three strangers rode into town from the south. Rufe was at the livery barn when they arrived. He was out back when he heard the unmistakable accents of Texas as one of the strangers asked the liveryman if the Circle L cow outfit was very far from town, because if it was the strangers, who had been in the saddle a long time would hole up overnight and look up the Circle L in the morning.

Rufe didn't hear the liveryman's reply, he hiked briskly up the alley and beat on the barred rear door of the jailhouse.

When Sheriff Corning opened the door he was frowning. Rufe pushed past, stopped in the office and related what he had heard and seen, and ended it with a shrewd assessment, 'Hired guns as sure as I'm standing here.'

Before the sheriff could speak, the youngest deputy arrived. He ignored Rufe. 'Sheriff, there's three Texans at the Palace askin' for directions to the Lefler place.'

As the deputies waited, the sheriff made his decision, yanked the gun-rack chain loose and handed each deputy a sawn-off scattergun, took the remaining one for himself and said, 'Let's hope Jonas's imports are still up there.'

They were, but they'd stopped at the café on the way. They were similar in some ways, none was any taller than the others, their clothing was faded and stained, they had no tie-down thongs over their holstered sidearms and hadn't shaved lately, nor had they bathed but that was inconsequential for the moment.

When the three lawmen pushed inside where Mark was getting ready to let down the chandeliers and light them, he stopped stone still and stared, as did the half-dozen or so regular customers.

Corning stopped just inside the door, Rufe on one side, the youngest deputy on the other side. The sheriff said, 'Drop 'em, gents. Real easy,' and cocked both hammers of his scattergun.

For several seconds after the three strangers faced around, there was neither movement nor sound. Rufe hauled back the dogs on his shotgun and the youngest deputy did the same.

A man didn't have to be a hired gunman to know his chances of survival at this moment were ten less than zero. One of the strangers dropped his beltgun. The other two followed his example. One of the strangers spoke quietly. 'Did we break a law, Sheriff?'

Corning didn't answer, he sent Rufe to see if the strangers had other weapons. They did have, each man had a short-barrelled, big bore belly-gun and two of them had boot knives.

Al Corning gestured with his shotgun for the strangers to leave the saloon. They obeyed to the letter and when Rufe poked one of them with his scattergun barrel he said, 'The middle of the road as far as the log building that says 'Sheriff' over the door.'

The poked man looked over his shoulder. 'Be careful with that dang thing. Sometimes they go off real easy.'

There were pedestrians, not many, but they watched the shotgun procession as long as they were in sight. Inside the jailhouse, the sheriff told the strangers to sit as he eased down both hammers of his weapon, went to the wall rack and racked it.

The man who had been poked said, 'That's not a neighbourly way to welcome folks to your town, Sheriff.'

Rufe and the youngest deputy kept their weapons. One of the strangers addressed the youngest deputy, 'Boy, you be careful with that thing. What's your name?'

Sheriff Corning said, 'Shut up,' went to his table, sat and leaned forward. 'I want your names,' he stated and none of the strangers hesitated. One said his name was Sam Houston, another said his name was William Barret Travis and the third one said, Joe Santa Anna.

The man who'd said his name was Travis was the same man Rufe had poked. They were all relaxed but the one calling himself Travis appeared the least concerned.

'If you got a charge,' he said, 'we'd like to hear it.'

Al Corning leaned back off his desk. 'You asked about the Circle L outfit.'

'Yes sir, for a fact.'

'That'd be Jonas Lefler.'

The spokesman nodded. 'Mister Lefler, is he a friend of yours, Sheriff?'

'I've known him for a long time. We're friends. He didn't tell me he'd sent for outside help.'

'Well now, Sheriff, you know how that is. Sometimes folks don't remember.' The Texan smiled. 'We'd admire to go up yonder an' get our guns. There's lots of thieves in this world.'

'You boys got a place to bed down tonight?'

'No sir, Sheriff. We only been in Laramie a couple of hours.' Corning arose, plucked the copper ring of cell locks from its hanger and said, 'I got good bunks for the night, gents.'

The three strangers stared hard. Sheriff Corning spoke again. 'Just until morning, gents. I got to be sure Jonas knows you.'

'He don't know us, Sheriff. He sent a letter to a friend of ours. He couldn't come because of the gout so he sent us.'

'On your feet, gents. Like I said, I got to talk to Mister Lefler. I'll ride out there first thing in the morning.'

Rufe leaned his shotgun aside and herded the Texans into the cell room. He put them all in the same cage and was locking the door when the man calling himself Travis said, 'No need for that, Deputy,' and Rufe made a wooden smile when he answered, 'We can't have you boys wanderin' around town until the sheriff's talked to Mister Lefler. There's two bunks an' a water pail. One of you can sleep on the floor.'

When Rufe returned to the office the youngest deputy was gone, which Rufe ignored as he showed one of his rare smiles when he said, 'Sheriff, you'd make a good preacher. You talk with a forked tongue.'

Corning had racked up the other two shotguns after removing their loads. He too was smiling as he went to his desk and sat down. 'I didn't exactly lie, Rufe. I *do* know Jonas Lefler. How'd they take being locked in?'

'Like scairt animals. That windy one's goin' to be in trouble with his friends tomorrow.' Rufe sat down. 'That was the easiest I ever saw three hired guns get taken. You want me along when you brace Lefler tomorrow?'

'Might be a good idea. He's a tad short-handed now.'

'Horace too, an' the kid?'

'Not the kid, Rufe, just you'n Horace.'

After the deputy's departure, the sheriff locked up from the outside and went up to his room. He was in good spirits; as Rufe had said, that had been almost too easy.

They didn't make the ride to Circle L in the morning because big Pete Moran walked in looking truculent. He ignored the deputies as he addressed the sheriff.

'I'm out three brindle steers. What're you goin' to do about it?'

'Did you track 'em?' the sheriff asked.

Moran shook his head. 'I haven't been able to hire riders an' if you think I'm goin' to sniff up three steers in that damned squatter country, you're crazy. I heard about them massacring three of Jonas's riders.'

Moran sat down in the chair beside the roadway door. His attitude was, as always, belligerent and disagreeable but to the men watching him he seemed to be working hard to keep up that image.

Rufe tried something when he said, 'There's a Texas gunman with the squatters. He's been teachin' them things. They did right well when Jonas's nightriders made the mistake of attackin' a place before it was dark. Another mistake was that this gunfightin' squatter was home with at least a dozen others when Jonas's hired hands charged by shootin' and hollerin'.'

Moran looked steadily at Rufe Kelly. 'They're bandin' together?'

'Sure seems like it, Mister Moran,' Rufe replied. 'I got a hunch they're goin' to start payin' back for lynchings and burnings. Have you ever been through a range war? Neither have I but sure as Gawd knows we got one now.'

Moran looked up at the sheriff. 'You got to send for soldiers.'

'I already did . . . they can't come.'

'Can't come for Chris' sake, that's what we pay taxes for isn't it?'

Corning nodded. 'Yes sir; but there's a shake-up from Washington. Soldiers are bein' reassigned, numbers are to be cut because folks in Washington think the army's too expensive.'

The large stockman gazed steadily at the sheriff in what seemed to be dumb silence for a long time then arose. 'Squatters shot up my house an' barn last night. I hid in the loft.'

Rufe said, 'You're lucky they didn't start fires.'

As though his deputy hadn't spoken, the sheriff said, 'Some advice, Mister Moran. Stay in town for awhile. Have you talked to Jonas lately?'

'No. I stayed close to my yard.'

Rufe looked disgusted but remained silent when the sheriff said, 'Settlers killed three Circle L riders who made a run on one of 'em. You want some advice; go to Denver or maybe even to Albuquerque and stay there.'

'Range war,' Moran mumbled. 'Jonas said there'd be a range war to wipe the squatters out.'

Sheriff Corning arose, went to the door and held it open. He did not say a word until the large man had departed, then he closed the door and looked at Rufe, who said, 'Gawddamned, big-mouthed bully. Watchin' him was like stickin' a pin in a baloon.'

194

The sheriff felt the same way but Moran wasn't the problem. He said, 'It's too late to make it out to Circle L an' back before dark. Tomorrow morning . . . ?'

Rufe arose. 'What about the Texas imports?'

'What about them?'

'You want to feed 'em?'

'Maybe tomorrow . . . then again maybe not. See you down at the livery about sun-up, Rufe.'

When the sheriff was about to leave, an elderly woman walked in. He knew her and nodded. The woman was not only diffident, she was clearly troubled. Her son was the youngest deputy. She didn't look at the sheriff when she said, 'My boy's taken down with the croup. Leastways that's what it looks like. I was on my way to the doctor's place, thought I'd let you know, Sheriff.' She brightened slightly. 'He's strong an' healthy; I'm sure he'll be up an' around in a few days. He likes workin' for you.'

The sheriff smiled. 'Doc'll look in on him. I'm sure you're right. He'll be fine in a few days. You tell him to mind Doc an' his mother.'

'Sheriff . . . ?'

'Yes'm.'

'He'll still have his job?'

The sheriff lied like a trooper. 'He'll still have it. I need good deputies an' he's one of the best.'

The elderly woman left beaming. The youngest deputy was her sole support.

Corning grinned dourly to himself, wagged his head and locked up from out front. Maybe, if the youngest deputy lived long enough, he'd make a passable lawman. Maybe.

As he was walking northward in settling gloom a horseman appeared from the north end of town. He was in no hurry, in fact this particular man did not know what the word hurry meant, never did anything that couldn't be accomplished in a measured and methodical manner.

The rider recognized the sheriff before he himself was recognized. He reined toward the plankwalk and said, 'No need for me to bed down out there with the chickens, Sheriff. That squatter's got guns beside every window.'

The 'breed deputy leaned on his saddlehorn. What he had just said consisted of more words spoken at one time than he usually spoke in a couple of days.

The lawman told him he, Horace King and Rufe Kelly were going out to the Lefler place in the morning and the impassive, dark-eyed deputy said nothing as he waited for the rest of it. It was a short wait, the sheriff told him he thought someone should be in town in case there was trouble.

The 'breed nodded and rode off without a word.

The sheriff hesitated when he was abreast of the Palace with all its lights glowing. A nightcap would be nice. He picked up the gait and continued up to the hotel and his room.

Sleep came quickly. This night he still had reason for anxiety but he also was becoming resigned to whatever fate or someone anyway, was ordaining. A man could do just so much.

He was for a damned fact on his own, had been on his own since the first lynching. It was a disappointment that the army wouldn't be coming and there had been other disappointments. He punched the pillow where he wanted it and went resignedly to sleep.

The wind was blowing when rattling windows awakened him when it was still dark. For a while he relished the warmth of his blankets until he eventually pushed up and sat on the edge of the bed in the dark.

Wind made wooden structures groan and move. It also blew roadway dust in which tiny stone pellets peppered both buildings and people.

As he buckled his britches, stamped into his boots and went out back to clean up he speculated for the hundredth time where a man could get work where the wind didn't blow.

When he was hiking southward in the direction of the livery barn where the hanging lamp was swinging, casting agitated light as far as the roadway, he saw Horace enter down there.

A person didn't have to be close to recognize the rawboned, tall deputy.

On the opposite side of the road, a flickering light came to life at the café. When the sheriff reached the barn, Rufe Kelly appeared out of darkness bundled into a sheep-pelt-lined horsehide coat. Rufe was never full of goodwill and cheerfulness before sunrise, and for a fact his mood only marginally improved after sunrise.

The liveryman's night hawk was bringing in horses when the sheriff arrived and exchanged nods with his deputies.

Evidently the hostler did not awaken before sunrise loaded with charitable thoughts. He asked the sheriff if he'd ever considered building a corral and shed near his office, and got no answer as the three lawmen put cold bits into the mouths of their horses, snugged up, led the horses to the roadway and mounted. If horses were going to pitch, and they didn't like being yanked out of a sound sleep either, a cold saddle blanket on their backs and a cold bit in their mouths could inspire them to do it. Ordinarily cranky saddle animals bogged their heads and bucked in a straight line. Even no more than an average rider could ride them out. Only the sunfishing sons of bitches that spun from side to side could get rid of whoever was on their backs.

Horace's ewe-necked, piggy-eyed, short-backed *grulla* faunched and got a hump under the saddle but he and Horace King were old associates. Horace wig-wagged the reins and growled. The tough mustang *grulla* put his head up, lost the hump and with his ears back awaited the next command from the two-legged thing on his back.

They had to buck wind all the way out of town. A mile or such a matter beyond where they left the road on the east side, the wind showed its capricious nature by swinging around and making them ride head first into it again.

Rufe grumbled to himself. Fortunately the wind whipped every word away the moment it came out. Horace looked over. He too was bundled, but Horace didn't have a horsehide coat, he had a Hudson's Bay garment that had originally reached slightly below the knees. Horace had cut a good foot off the bottom.

Sheriff Corning rode in silence. If he'd wanted to talk he would have had to shout. He didn't want to talk.

The sun came halfway and seemed to hang there, daunted by the wind. The three horsemen picked up tantalizing wisps of cook-stove smoke a half-hour before there was enough light for them to make out distant lights and eventually the outlines of buildings.

Horace reined close to Rufe and leaned. 'You reckon the old bastard'll invite us to breakfast?'

Rufe looked back irritably and did not say a word.

The wind did accomplish something of questionable merit, it prevented dogs from catching man and horse scent until the three lawmen were entering the yard.

For a time there was no response, men in their warm and snug bunkhouse could convince themselves the dogs had scented-up a varmint, a foraging skunk or possibly scavenging coyotes. In any case no one even cracked the door until the lawmen had put their animals inside the barn out of the wind and were crossing the yard.

The bunkhouse door was swiftly closed.

At the main house there were only two lights, one in the kitchen, the other one in the parlour. Recalling Horace's remark about breakfast, Rufe said, 'Whatever Jonas cooks I'm pretty sure I never been that hungry,' and as they approached close he also said, 'Skinflint; he could hire a woman to cook an' clean up.'

The barking became louder and more insistent as they mounted the steps to the porch. When the sheriff raised a gloved fist to knock the door was abruptly yanked inward and Jonas Lefler, horse pistol in his right hand, recoiled in total surprise at the sight of three unsmiling lawmen in front of him.

The sheriff dryly said, 'Good morning, Jonas.'

The squinty-eyed older man let go a long breath before speaking. 'Come inside.'

There was a small fire in the fireplace, the parlour was chilly, Lefler had his boots and britches on but the tops of his long red underwear was where a shirt should have been. He considered the three lawmen. 'Which one of you can cook?' he asked and got three head wags. He put the big old horse pistol on a table and jerked his head as he led the way to the kitchen. He spoke over his shoulder, 'What do you want?'

'Talk,' the sheriff said, loosening his coat and pocketing his gloves.

Jonas had been frying something; with his back to his callers he said, 'Set. Coffee'll be hot directly. Sheriff, there's nothin' to talk about. What in hell you doin' ridin' around in the dark?'

They sat at a round table with one short leg that made the table tilt when someone leaned on it.

Horace said, 'That smells good, what is it?' and got a glare from the cowman at the stove. 'Fried mush. Somethin' wrong with your nose? Fried mush don't smell good. Al, coffee's boilin', fill the cups.'

As the sheriff arose to obey Lefler turned on him. Before the older man could speak the sheriff said, 'Pete Moran came by. His hands quit, he lost some critters an' he's afraid to leave his yard.'

Jonas snorted. 'Big, overgrown puss-gut. He's always made a lot of noise and snarled. Al, he's a lily-livered son of a bitch. In a pinch he's as useless as teats on a man.'

Jonas brought two platters of dark-brown fried mush patties to the table, got a jar of something as clear as water and put it on the table too. It was sugar water.

There was no butter and the coffee tasted like the floor of a tipi where the inhabitants went barefoot.

As Jonas sat down he said, 'Well, eat!'

Horace was the first, then the sheriff. The last man to spear some fried mush cakes was Rufe Kelly who'd had to eat those things when he'd been a child because there was nothing else, and when he left home he promised himself he would never eat fried mush again as long as he lived.

He speared two, slathered them with sugar water and ate. Jonas Lefler's hoe cakes were fried so hard not even sugar water would penetrate them.

11

Angry Men

While they were eating, the sheriff said, 'I got your three Texans locked up.'

Jonas paused with a fork in mid-air and spoke waspishly. 'My three Texans? What're you talkin' about?'

'You wrote down there but the hired gun you wrote to was down with the gout so he passed it along to the three cock roosters I locked up last night.'

Jonas ate furiously for a while before spearing the sheriff with one of his squinty-eyed, venomous glares. 'They're a dime a dozen.'

Corning ate for a few moments then gravely inclined his head. 'You're right, they're a dime a dozen, but Jonas, suppose you couldn't hire any more?'

The pair of older men looked steadily at each other. Jonas said, 'Are you

206

threatenin' me, Sheriff? Because if you are I don't scare worth a . . . '

'It's not a threat,' the sheriff retorted. 'It's a promise. That's why we come out here so early.'

Jonas put down his eating utensils. 'Sheriff, let's quit talkin' in riddles. I'm a simple man. I say straight out what I got to say an' expect others to do likewise.'

The sheriff leaned back. 'Those was about as good a set of hoe cakes as I've ever eaten,' he said, and Jonas continued to look disturbed, more suspiciously baffled than cranky. 'I never made a decent mush cake in my life. Ask the lads at the bunkhouse. When I invite 'em up here to eat with me, you never heard such alibi-ing in your life.'

'Why did you lynch Hewlett?'

This time the cowman was completely caught off balance. 'Why did . . . ? I never hung no one in my life, an' you can believe it or not.'

Corning smiled a little. 'I believe

you,' he said. 'That twenty-dollar gold piece you give Kellogg; what was that for, attackin' that settler up near the foothills?'

Jonas put his eating utensils aside and pushed the platter away. Horace and Rufe continued to eat as though each of them was hearing impaired.

Jonas bristled, his squinty eyes showed fire. 'You come out here to make trouble. I know you, Al. There's men at the bunkhouse if you're here for a fight.'

The sheriff was not only calm, he took advantage of the cowman's irascibility. 'I can prove Kellogg killed that squatter named Snelling. I can prove you sent your nightriders to attack the Bertram place.'

'Who? I never heard of anyone named . . . '

'Jonas, next time you're in town ask Mark Turner who shot three candles out of their holders. Ask Doc how your nightriders got picked off like birds on a fence — off runnin' horses while they was shootin' up the Bertram place. One more thing, Jonas, an' you better think about this: the settler named Bertram is making a squatter army; he's the one who can outshoot anyone you know an' more 'n likely your three Texans thrown in.'

Lefler only picked out one segment of what the sheriff had said. He snorted derisively, 'Squatter army? When us cowmen get through there won't be a one of 'em left.'

Sheriff Corning watched his deputies use bandannas to wipe their faces and push empty plates aside. He said, 'Ready to ride, boys?' and stood up. 'Rufe, go with Jonas when he puts a shirt on. An' a coat, the wind's cold out there.'

Rufe arose but Lefler did not; he looked up and snarled, 'I got some good men at the bunkhouse.'

The sheriff reached, yanked the smaller and older man to his feet and shoved him toward Rufe. He said, 'Jonas, I give you every chance, now you old bastard, I'm goin' to lock you up an' feed the key to a turkey.'

Lefler sputtered. 'When my lawyer gets back from Cheyenne we'll see . . .'

'Take him, Rufe.'

The dour, husky deputy shoved Jonas Lefler and when the cowman would have turned in defiance, Rufe got a handful of red underwear, lifted Lefler off his feet and threw him. Jonas fetched up against the stone sides of his fireplace and grimaced in pain. Rufe was not ordinarily a sympathetic individual. He pulled Lefler away from the stone and raised a fist. Jonas crouched and moved swiftly toward a dark room.

Horace arose. 'Them hoe cakes wasn't bad. You want me to go talk to those fellers at the bunkhouse?'

The sheriff nodded. 'Be careful, Horace.'

When the sheriff was the only one remaining in the kitchen he filled his coffee cup half full, tipped in some of the sugar water and went out into the parlour to drink the mixture, but it was too sweet so he put the cup aside. Rufe and Jonas appeared, the cowman wearing a wool shirt and a buckskin coat from which the fringes had been cut off. The coat was lined with coarse red flannel.

Jonas plucked a battered old stained hat off an antler rack, pulled it down hard and glared. He was going to speak when the wind carried sounds of a commotion down at the bunkhouse.

Corning pushed Jonas ahead out into the yard. The three of them went as far as the bunkhouse where the sheriff entered with a cocked gun in his right fist.

Two rangemen were helping a third one to his feet. He had a bloody mouth and Horace said, 'Sheriff, we got one bushy-tailed one an' two sensible ones.'

The rangemen were herded to the barn with their employer. Horses were brought in to be saddled and the rider Horace had struck paused twice to wipe his mouth. No one said a word.

The wind had lost some of its velocity but it made up for this by changing direction, striking the cavalcade of Circle L riders head-on, then from one side, the other side and from the rear.

One of the unhappy Lefler riders said, 'Folks should've let the In'ians keep this damned country.'

No one agreed nor disagreed but up front, where Jonas was riding stirrup with the sheriff, the cowman said, 'When my fee lawyer gets back . . . I ain't goin' with you willingly. There'll be a law . . . '

The sheriff gravely inclined his head. 'There's likely a law, but Jonas, they're goin' to lynch you sure as I'm ridin' with you. I'm protectin' you. There's likely a law about that too.'

The cowman turned his head. 'An army of squatters? There ain't enough left in the country for that.'

Sheriff Corning had to lean to make himself understood when he answered. 'All they need is one gun-savvy settler teachin' the others. When they're ready they could carry your damned war to your yard, kill you an' burn what's left . . . Jonas, I tried to prevent this; you wouldn't listen. They'll likely put more'n a gold piece worth twenty dollars on your head. They'll kill you if they can. I'll bet new money on it.'

By the time they reached town both men and horses were exhausted from being buffeted by wind. There were no people on the plankwalks and where wood stoves were heating homes, the smoke barely left chimneys before it was bent flat with ridge poles.

The jailhouse was cold. Horace went to build a fire. Someone yelled from the cell room. The sheriff ignored that as he told the cowman and his riders to shed their coats and empty their pockets on his table. The rangemen obeyed but Jonas hung back snarling until Rufe Kelly came up behind, lifted Jonas as he'd done at the ranch and asked if the sheriff wanted him turned upside down so his pockets would empty themselves.

Corning shook his head and Rufe put the smaller and less heavy man down. The sheriff pointed to his table without saying a word. Lefler shuffled over and emptied his pockets.

The sheriff told Lefler to stay where he was and had the deputies herd the rangemen into the cell-room to be locked in. For as long as the cell-room door was open the bawling and cursing of the Texans was clearly audible. After Rufe and Horace returned to the office and closed the thick oaken door, the bawling was barely audible.

The sheriff leaned on the front of his desk eyeing Jonas Lefler. The cowman was as defiant as usual but shifted often where he sat and when the sheriff did not speak, Lefler finally did.

'A squatter posse,' he said scornfully. 'You got any idea how many cattlemen'll respond if there's a war? All the way from Wyoming; they got a sheep war goin' on up there.'

'Jonas,' the sheriff said quietly, 'when

you'n your riders took Hewlett out an' hung him you saved me from havin' to rack him.'

'I didn't hang Hewlett!'

The sheriff gravely nodded. 'You knew it would happen. As long as I had Hewlett, if he told me all he knew . . . Who else would hang the worthless bastard?'

Lefler reverted to their earlier discussion. 'There'll be cowmen come from all over. Squatter army? They'll hang 'em, shoot 'em or burn 'em out.'

The sheriff went around to sit behind his table. 'Jonas, get it through your pig-stubborn head; if the stockmen gather like you think they'll do, what about the hundreds of settlers?'

Jonas shifted on the bench again before speaking. 'They won't gather, they're too scairt.'

The sheriff wagged his head. 'You damned old fool; it won't matter whether they gather or not. You make a war here an' it'll be in every newspaper in the country. An' you'll wish to hell you'd never been born.'

Lefler jack-knifed up to his feet and went to stand by the cell-room door. 'Lock me up. When my fee lawyer gets back he'll get me out an' no matter what it costs me, Al, I'll nail your hide to my barn wall!'

The sheriff arose slowly, took Lefler to an empty cell, locked him in and when the three Texans yelled he told them they'd be fed and returned to the office.

Rufe was gone but Horace was still there. He said Rufe had gone to the eatery.

Sheriff Corning sat, considered Horace for a long moment before saying, 'Stubborn old bastard.'

Horace agreed. 'Don't let him out or sure as hell he'll try to round up the ranchers like he said.'

The sheriff leaned back off his table. 'They'll kill him sure as we're sittin' here, an' as far as I know they got a right to. They know who he is, that he's behind all their misery.'

'Keep him locked up,' Horace said again, and the sheriff's response was brief. 'His fee lawyer'll get him out with some kind of writ. Horace, go over to the café, get three buckets of stew or hash and feed them noisy Texans.'

While Horace was gone the sheriff went up to the Palace where the barman Mark Turner set up a bottle and a small jolt glass, looked at the lawman and leaned to speak in a lowered voice although there were only two other men at the bar and they were down where the bar turned to reach the wall.

'That rough-lookin', unwashed squatter's in town. The one that shot out my candles,' and as the sheriff straightened up, Turner told him the rest of it. 'With five other squatters. They was in here for a drink an' left.'

The sheriff returned to the roadway. There was no sign of squatters. He went to the jailhouse where Horace and the Texans were arguing, returned to the roadway and hiked as far as the livery barn where the proprietor spoke before the sheriff could. 'Six of them raggedy-pants squatters left their horses in the corral out back. Sheriff, every man-jack of 'em was wearin' a belt-gun on the outside of their coats.'

'What did they say?'

'A tall feller with shaggy hair told me to fork feed the horses and they'd pay me when they come back.' The liveryman paused. 'That's all. The others never said a word, but I can tell from experience they ain't in town for no May Day celebration.'

'Where would they be now?'

'I got no idea. Six of 'em, Sheriff.'

Wherever the squatters were for the time being was less important than rounding up the deputies. He found Rufe with Horace at the jailhouse where for a change there was no noise from the cell room. Three empty grub buckets were stacked near the door. Corning sent Rufe to find the 'breed and bring him to the jailhouse after he told the pair of deputies what he'd heard at the Palace.

Rufe arose but made no move toward the door. He said, 'That big one's with 'em?' and when the sheriff nodded Rufe said, 'Then I'd better stay in here. If they're here for trouble . . . we don't need the 'breed anyway.'

Before the sheriff could repeat his order, Arthur Fleming came in acting breathless and upset. 'There's a posse of squatters in town, Sheriff. Six of 'em armed to the gullet. They bought some sausage and bread at the store an' before they left they stood at the front window lookin' over here. I think you'd better round up the town vigilantes.'

Sheriff Corning's attitude was in marked contrast to the agitated condition of the storekeeper. 'Go on back, Arthur. We know they're in town.'

'Sheriff, for Gawd's sake . . . '

'Go back to the store, Arthur!' As the

sheriff said this he went to the roadway door and held it open.

The merchant left looking both ways as he crossed the road. Horace grinned without speaking. Rufe built and lighted a quirly and spoke through exhaled smoke. 'If I was in your boots, Sheriff, I'd give 'em Lefler. Otherwise all hell's goin' to bust loose.'

Corning did not even consider Rufe's suggestion but he made a bitter, small smile as he returned to the chair behind his table. If he'd been between a rock and a hard place before . . . Damn Jonas Lefler! If he hadn't brought him and his rangemen to town as sure as Gawd made green grass Bertram would have taken his settlers to the Lefler place and would have lynched Jonas and as many of the Circle L riders as they could find.

Sheriff Corning thumbed back his hat and exchanged a long look with his deputies. Fate had dealt him a loser's hand for a fact. He was now protecting the one individual in the Laramie country who was responsible for the kind of trouble that was going to land squarely in someone's lap. Not Lefler's lap, Sheriff Corning's lap.

12

Choices

The unexpected happened. Lefler's fee lawyer from Cheyenne arrived on the Cheyenne to Laramie stage. If he noticed anything unusual, which he probably didn't because his objective was the jailhouse, he gave no sign of it as he came in looking troublesome, ignored the deputies, stopped in front of the sheriff's table and flung down a folder paper. He said, 'Read it, Mister Corning. It's a bail bond in the sum of five hundred dollars for the release of Jonas Lefler.'

The sheriff didn't touch the paper. He looked at the younger man as he said, 'How'd you know Jonas was here?'

'I went by the ranch. There wasn't a soul there so I came here. You've got him haven't you?'

The sheriff did not answer, he unfolded the paper and read it slowly, put it flat down on his desk and said, 'Have a seat, Mister Ballester.'

The lawyer did not move. 'You didn't answer my question; do you have Mister Lefler locked up?'

'Yes, I have him locked up. *Sit down!*'

The lawyer sat without changing his truculent expression. The sheriff said, 'There's a crowd of squatters in town. If I hand him over to you they'll hang him.' Corning tapped the paper on his desk. 'I'll honour this thing even though it's an out-of-state writ. You can have Jonas, and ten minutes after you take him out of here them squatters will hang him, an' maybe you too. You want him? Rufe, bring Jonas up.'

As Rufe arose the lawyer held up a hand. 'Wait a bit. I didn't see any settlers out there.'

'Would you know 'em if you saw

'em? Take my word for it, friend, they're out there.'

'Do they know Mister Lefler is in here?'

The sheriff shrugged. 'By now I'd guess they know. They could ask around town.'

Ballester glanced briefly at the stone-faced silent deputies before speaking again. 'What are you going to do?'

'With Lefler? Hold him until a judge arrives, which may be next week or next month. Mister, my jailhouse is the safest place for him. Go around town, go to the Palace saloon, to the general store. Ask around, talk to folks. If you still want him when you come back you can have him.'

Again the lawyer looked at the silent, hard-faced deputies before speaking. He required that much time to make a decision. He had come to the jailhouse office full of confidence and defiance. According to the law he had right on his side. What he had walked into was something which had precious little to do with written law.

He leaned back against the wall looking anything but confident or belligerent. Sheriff Corning gave him no opportunity to speak. He said, 'Mister Ballester, to be right frank with you, Jonas and I've been friends and un-friends ever since I came here. He's been troublesome most of that time. If those men hang the old bastard I tell you straight out, it'll make my job a lot easier.'

The lawyer said, 'They wouldn't bother me. They don't even know who I am,' and Rufe snorted before saying, 'By now they know who you are and what you are, but, even if they didn't an' you walked out of here with Mister Lefler I wouldn't give a counterfeit cartwheel you wouldn't end up hangin' alongside Mister Lefler.'

The sheriff inadvertently ended this discussion when he said, 'If you want to talk to Jonas I'll fetch him to the office.'

Ballester sprang to his feet. 'No!

Some other time maybe,' and departed so quickly Horace laughed. Rufe didn't, he said, 'Book-learnt son of a bitch. Sheriff, I got an idea. Maybe we could find one of them squatters an' bring him in here to talk.'

Horace looked around. 'What good would that do? They most likely figure the time for talkin' is past, an' I think so too.'

Rufe lapsed into silence. He rolled and lighted another smoke and only looked up when the Sheriff said, 'You lads stay here. Lock the door an' get a pair of scatterguns. I'll be back directly.'

The scent of trouble had the town quiet with very few people in the roadway. Up at the Palace when the sheriff walked in, Mark Turner, in the act of drawing off a stein of beer for a customer, froze. So did the half-dozen or so other patrons of the saloon.

The sheriff didn't see the three men at a distant card table, he went directly to the bar where Turner jerked his head sideways without speaking. Corning turned. The three men at the poker table were looking back. Sheriff Corning spoke to the barman. 'A bottle and a glass, Mark,' and when these were set up the sheriff took them and approached the poker table. The three seated men were impassive. They had shellbelts and holstered sidearms around old unwashed barn coats. Only one wore a stockman's hat, the other two were hatless.

The sheriff kicked around a chair, sat down, put the bottle in the centre of the table along with the jolt glass and said, 'Help yourself, gents.'

No one reached for the bottle as they impassively regarded the lawman. Sheriff Corning tried another approach. 'Lefler's locked in a cell at the jailhouse, if that's who you been lookin' for.'

The tallest of the settlers finally spoke. 'On what charge?'

'Suspicion of murder for openers,' Corning replied, and leaned forward on the table. 'If you gents had some idea of lynching him, I'll tell you straight out, you'll get yourselves killed.'

The tall man named Bertram addressed the sheriff again. 'Mister, I was seven years a Texas Ranger. I know you can't hold him on somethin' as weak as suspicion for long.'

Corning smiled slightly at the tall squatter. 'An' you gents'll wait. I can hold him for as long as I got to.' He looked steadily at the former Texas lawman. 'Protective custody. Look it up. Gents, have a drink on me an' let's talk reason.'

Without another word the tall man arose, jerked his head and led his companions out of the saloon. Sheriff Corning had a drink by himself, took the bottle and glass back to the bar, put silver beside the bottle, nodded to Turner and also left the saloon.

The doors hadn't quite stopped swinging when one of the Palace's regulars said, 'Them stump-jumpers need a lesson. Seems like we'd ought to call out the vigilantes.'

Mark Turner scowled. 'Leave it be. Al Corning can handle it.'

He got several doubting looks but the vigilante idea was not mentioned again, possibly because some of the men at the bar were vigilantes and they had no stomach for a shoot-out. It was one thing to run down a cow or horsethief, it was something altogether different to get into a stand-up fight out in the roadway, and by now most of them knew who that tall squatter was and how deadly he was with a six-gun.

As the sheriff was bucking a rising wind on his way to the jailhouse, the squatter named Wayne Dunning emerged from shadows beside the jailhouse and spoke swiftly. 'They're goin' to set fire to the jailhouse. They want Lefler to burn like he burnt some of them.'

The sheriff twisted to look up and down the roadway. There were lights but no pedestrains nor horsemen, the wind was increasing and from long habit the folks of Laramie got in

229

where it couldn't buffet them. He said, 'Thanks,' and was turning away when a second shadow, shorter and thicker came out of the dusky early evening. This man, whom the sheriff recognized as Jake Holzer, made no attempt to lower his voice when he said, 'You want to keep from gettin' burnt out? In this wind the whole town'll go up. You want to prevent it?'

Corning looked steadily at the shorter and stockier man. 'How?' he asked.

'You sneak Lefler out into the alley an' I'll guarantee you they'll never catch him.'

Corning eyed the grim, unsmiling man. 'They'll run you down no matter how fast your farm horses are, Mister Holzer.'

A wild gust of wind spewed roadway dust from the north end of town to the south end. The liveryman's outside hanging lamp swung wildly until a particular gust caught it tipped, went down the mantle and blew out the lighted wick.

Neither of the settlers did more than lower their heads and brace into the wind. Sheriff Corning expectorated. He had been speaking when the roadway dust passed. Holzer raised his head and said, 'He'll be safer than in your jailhouse an' when things has settled we'll give him back to you.'

Dunning nodded his head. 'We can do it, Sheriff, as Gawd's my witness, but if you get stubborn they'll burn down the whole town if they got to, you'n your deputies inside an' other folks as well. In weather like this . . . Sheriff, they're not goin' to give up. They want Lefler. They aim to get him. They figure to hang him in the middle of town.'

The sheriff gazed dispassionately at the pair of settlers. 'Like I said, they'll ride you down.'

Holzer shook his head. 'There isn't a horse born that can catch us. Sheriff, you want to keep Lefler alive? Bring him to the back alley. If you get pigheaded or waste more time . . . Sheriff, on a night like this if they set fire to your jailhouse the wind'll carry the fire everywhere. Give us Lefler then let 'em see you don't have him.'

'An' you hand him over to the lynchers. Gents, it was a good idea but I'd be crazy to hand Lefler over to squatters.'

Holzer responded brusquely. 'You don't have no choice. When it's over we'll bring him back alive. Dig in your heels an' Laramie'll be burnt to the ground come morning.'

Another of those capricious gusts of wind swept from the north end of town down through and out the south end. This time the wind not only blew hard it also was cold.

The tall settler turned away. Holzer hesitated. 'Bring Lefler out to the alley. They'll be comin' with torches an' guns directly.'

Sheriff Corning squinted at the shorter, stocky man, turned to enter the jailhouse when another gust made him bend into it.

Rufe was by the little roadway window. When the sheriff came in Rufe said, 'It looked like you met someone out there.'

Sheriff Corning went over beside Rufe as he explained what the men he had met wanted him to do. While they were talking, a man yelling up near the Palace could be heard in the jailhouse, thanks to the north-south wind.

Horace went to yank the chain loose at the gun rack. While he was doing this the sheriff said, 'Son of a bitch!'

Horace left the gun rack, crossed to the window and froze. 'Damned idiots,' he exclaimed. 'Them torches they're carryin'll sure as hell start fires.' He straightened up looking at the sheriff. 'There's more'n six.'

Corning shook his head like a bull in fly time, took down his brass key ring and went to the cell-room door before speaking. 'Rufe, go look out into the alley.'

Rufe turned to look at the sheriff.

'Why? They're out there with their firebrands too?'

'Gawddammit, Rufe, just go look out there. If you see a couple of men come back.'

A howling wind caught at the jailhouse eaves and the building groaned. When the sheriff brought Jonas Lefler to the office, Rufe was standing in the store-room doorway. 'I saw a shadow out there. Looked like a squatter. I didn't see anythin' else.'

'What's he doing?'

'Over against the fence across the alley . . . Sheriff?'

Corning said, 'Horace, watch those idiots with the firebrands. They're goin' to try an' set the jailhouse on fire.' He gave Jonas Lefler a hard shove in Rufe's direction. 'Take him out back an' give him to that squatter.'

Rufe stared.

'Rufe, *do it!*'

The deputy didn't move. 'That's a squatter, Sheriff. He's one of 'em. I thought we meant to keep that old

234

bastard alive.' The sheriff caught Lefler by the scruff from behind, shouldered Rufe Kelly out of the way, went to the alley door, lifted the *tranca* away and opened the door.

It was dark. Jonas twisted in the lawman's grip until the sheriff shook him hard and shoved him outside where the wind was as strong as it had been most of the day. Lefler swore and tried to use his fists. The sheriff half pushed, half carried him into the alley where a second shadow came from the south side of the jailhouse. This settler was large and strong. He grabbed the cowman, jerked him away from the sheriff as the shorter, stockier settler came forward. From the jailhouse doorway Rufe said, 'They're goin' to hang him.'

Sheriff Corning watched until he could no longer see the struggling man between the other two then went back inside, barred the door and glared at his deputy. 'If they do they won't set no fires. It might not be a decent trade but I think it is.'

Horace called. Corning and Rufe Kelly returned to the office which was now lighted by a variety of glare that was unsteadily wind-whipped.

Horace had a Winchester from the wall rack. The sheriff went to lean down beside him and look out.

'It's more'n six,' Horace said. 'They stopped out front.'

They had indeed stopped in the centre of the road. One torch-bearer left the others to approach the jailhouse. By the flaring torches, the men inside recognized him. It was the tall settler named Bertram. When he reached the door he struck it with the butt of his six-gun.

Sheriff Corning stood to one side of the door as he raised his voice and said, 'You damned fools better douse them firebrands.'

Bertram called back. 'We will when you give us your prisoner.'

Corning's answer was brusque. 'Put

them torches out an' you can come in.'

This time Bertram's call was delayed. 'Show us Lefler.'

'Can't do that,' the sheriff called back. 'Douse them torches an' you can come inside.'

The squatters were not in a bargaining mood. Bertram made a menacing reply. 'We're goin' to burn your jailhouse, Sheriff, with you in it unless you give us Lefler.'

Horace cocked his Winchester, something the men outside couldn't hear but which the sheriff and Rufe heard. Corning scowled. 'Ease down the dog, Horace.'

'If you let 'em in they'll hang the three of us when they don't find Lefler.'

'*Ease the dog down real easy, Horace!*'

The deputy obeyed but not in good spirit, and for a fact he could be right, if the lynchers found Lefler was gone they just might take out their frustration on the lawmen.

Bertram called again. 'Shove him out front, Sheriff. You'n your deputies stay inside. Sheriff? It's cold out here. *Shove him out!*'

Even though the wind was blowing from north to south an unearthly racket from the vicinity of the livery barn near the southern end of town did not cause more than a brief diversion. It was loud and sounded like a heavy wagon. A few men turned to squint into the southerly darkness, they were individuals who had either freighted or had in other ways worked with large outfits.

Whatever the diversion occasioned in these men, Bertram's final shout brought their attention back to the jailhouse. Bertram's call was loud, even so if he hadn't been standing close to the door the words would have been swept southward by the wind.

'This is your last chance, Sheriff. Shove Lefler out here or we'll burn the place down with you in it. *Hand him over!*'

At the door, Corning looked in the direction of his deputies. They looked back, unrelentingly defiant. They would fight to their last breath whatever the odds. The sheriff considered the door and reached for the heavy wooden bar in its hangers on both sides. Bertram might set the jailhouse afire but he would never get inside unless the *tranca* was lifted.

The deputies stood transfixed as the sheriff leaned with one hand on the heavy wooden door-bar as he called to Bertram.

'Only a couple of you can come in. All right?'

Bertram's shout came back short and clearly audible. 'There's three of you in there. I'll come in with three settlers.'

Horace and Rufe were like statues as the sheriff slowly lifted the *tranca*. When the door was no longer blocked, Horace gripped the Winchester in both hands but did not cock it.

When Bertram entered with his torch

a shorter man was behind him. He too had a lighted firebrand. Smoke spread where there was no wind to dispel it. The sheriff said, 'Put those torches out,' and nodded toward the bucket of drinking water.

The pair of settlers quenched the firebrands. The oily smoke had been too much for them too.

Bertram eyed Horace with his carbine and Rufe standing poised with his tie-down thong hanging loose. He faced the sheriff. 'You want to fetch the old bastard up here or do we do it?'

Sheriff Corning tossed the key ring to Bertram and stood mute as the pair of settlers flung back the door, disappeared in the gloomy cell room and returned looking murderous. Bertram said, 'Where is he?'

Corning answered truthfully. 'I don't know.'

Bertram shifted his attention to the deputies. 'Where's he hid?'

Rufe said nothing. Horace might

have but the sheriff spoke. 'Search the place, Mister Bertram.'

The former lawman growled for one of his companions to look in the store room. As this was being done, Bertram looked icily at Sheriff Corning. 'You'll tell us if we got to put your bare feet into a fire.'

Corning repeated it. 'I don't know where he is. If I did know I'd most likely not tell you, but I don't know an' that's a fact.'

'You had him in here, Sheriff.'

The short settler completed his search and faced Bertram shaking his head. Bertram told him to go out to the others and make a search in the vicinity of the jailhouse, and anywhere else they figured the fugitive might be.

Corning added something. 'An' tell 'em to douse those torches. With the wind blowin' one spark an' Laramie'll be ashes come daylight.'

Bertram growled at the shorter settler. 'Douse 'em, Eli. Use lanterns.'

'We don't have no lanterns,' the short man said.

'Get 'em,' Bertram growled. 'If you got to kick in some doors, get 'em!'

After the short settler left, Bertram turned on the sheriff. 'We're goin' to get him if we got to search every house, henhouse an' cellar in Laramie.'

Horace went to put wood in the little pot-bellied stove, with the roadway door ajar it was cold. Rufe remained by the window with an expression of frank hostility. His tie-down thong was hanging loose. The sheriff worried; Rufe was fearless. From what he knew about Bertram there wasn't anyone in the territory who could match him with a sidearm.

It was close to dawn when a couple of cold and dispirited settlers came to the jailhouse to tell Bertram they had searched every place a man could hide and had turned up nothing but some irate townsmen they'd disturbed.

For the first time since entering the jailhouse, Bertram went to a wall bench and sat down looking steadily at the sheriff.

He said, 'I can kill you,' and the sheriff gravely inclined his head without speaking.

Bertram turned his attention first on Rufe whose expression told the big settler all he had to know. Next he considered Horace and got a believable head wag. 'I got no idea where Lefler is. None at all.'

'He was locked in!' Bertram exclaimed, and Horace nodded his head without speaking.

'An' those Circle L riders of his is locked up down the hall.'

Horace nodded again without speaking.

Bertram's temper flared. He arose from the bench. 'All right. Take off your boots. One at a time I'll shove your feet into the stove.'

Rufe spoke coldly. 'The sheriff isn't no liar. Neither is Horace, neither am I. Mister, we told you Gawd's truth. We don't know where Lefler is.'

'How did he get out of his cell?'

He got no answer from the three lawmen.

'Take off your boots!'

Sheriff Corning said, 'I let him out about an hour ago.'

'Where did he go?'

'That's what none of us know. I let him out the back door in the alley.'

Bertram sank down on the bench again, this time looking from one lawman to the other. Horace risked an opinion. 'If your men couldn't find him maybe he hightailed it for the ranch.'

Bertram considered that in long silence, arose without a word and stalked out into the wind-scoured roadway where some of his companions were loitering. He told them to get their horses.

Sheriff Corning stood in the jailhouse doorway. He and Bertram exchanged a look before mounted settlers appeared, one leading a big roman-nosed horse with feathers on each ankle. Bertram took the reins to this animal, swung up and led the way out of Laramie. He and his riders had to brace into the north wind until they came to the Circle L cutoff, then the wind hit them on the left side.

13

Holzer's Invention

When dawn came, the wind was still blowing but with noticeably less force. Horace kept the stove fed. The log jailhouse had been chinked but that had been a long time ago and wherever the chinking had fallen out wind came in between the logs.

The sheriff was tired; he hadn't done anything physical to make him that way, but he was nonetheless tired as he sat at his table.

Horace said, 'They'll find him if he's out there an' my guess is that's where he went; the only place he's been safe for half his lifetime.'

Sheriff Corning indifferently nodded. 'When the wind lets up we'll ride out an' cut him down.' He looked from one deputy to the other. 'If that'll end it . . .'

Rufe nodded. He was in total agreement. Without Jonas Lefler to keep the pot boiling things would settle down — hopefully. Big, mouthy, bullying Moran had been broke to lead. There would be other stockmen who, without a leader, would grumble and growl a lot but as a leaderless group . . .

The man who managed the corralyard for the stage company, whose name was Jack, brought a gust of wind with him, and had to lean to close the roadway door after himself. It would have been normal if he'd made some exasperated comment about the weather; instead he faced the sheriff when he said, 'My northbound from down yonder came in with a busted door an' two crippled horses.'

The lawmen listened dispassionately. There were always accidents.

'There was two passengers, one a travellin' man an' the other a snake-oil peddler. But for them gents they'd've never got the animals out of their tangled harness and got the coach back upright.'

Now, the sheriff and his deputies showed interest. If one of them'd had in mind asking for an explanation, the upset corralyard boss allowed no interruption.

'Crazy; I didn't believe it but there was the proof in my yard along with the driver an' them passengers. I wouldn't have guessed . . . '

Rufe finally got a word in. 'Guessed what?'

'The wind was blowin' real hard. My whip seen it comin' and figured to drive off the road. It was comin' too fast an' the horses went crazy.'

Rufe interrupted. 'What was comin' too fast?'

The corralyard boss switched his attention from the sheriff to the deputy. 'You won't believe,' he said, and Rufe's temper flared.

'Try us. For once in your life try the

truth. What're you talkin' about?'

'It was a wagon, sort of like a heavy ranch wagon an' it was comin' down the middle of the road faster'n my whip ever saw anythin' move. A wagon with a sail planted some way near the back end. There was two squatters, a big 'un an' a shorter one. The whip said they was both up front with a rudder that turned the front wheels. He said the horses left the road, rearin' an' squawlin' an' tipped the stage over. By the time him'n the passengers climbed around an' got to their feet the contraption was almost out of sight headin' for Hebersburg.'

The corralyard man went to a chair and slumped. 'Them passengers along with the whip swore to me about what they saw. The travellin' peddler who got an ankle hurt when the coach went over, said no one would ever believe 'em. He said when a man pondered on it, that contraption was goin' like the wind with no horses on it.'

Rufe made a dry remark. 'With a sail like a boat?'

The corralyard boss nodded.

After the corralyard man left, Horace sat wagging his head. 'He's right about one thing, no one's goin' to believe it; a horseless wagon travellin' faster'n horses with a boat sail stepped in its floor. Who in the hell . . . ?'

Thus far the sheriff hadn't said much. Now he did. 'Them two squatters I gave Lefler to . . . they said whatever it was a horse couldn't catch it. Lefler won't be at his ranch. Maybe down at Hebersburg?'

Horace went to stand by the window, but only briefly. The café's roadway window was steamed. He said he was hungry and left the sheriff and Rufe Kelly alone. A fair amount of time had passed; Rufe, who was not a fast thinker, said, 'Wasn't one of them squatters you talked to the one named Holzer?'

Corning nodded.

Rufe arose, cleared his throat, regarded

the sheriff stoically for a moment, then laughed, something he almost never did. 'A wind wagon, Sheriff. I'm goin' over to the eatery.'

The sheriff remained at his table. Something as revolutionary as a wagon being driven by the wind . . . He rummaged for his whiskey bottle, had two pulls and put the bottle away. Who in the hell would get such an idea; the damned wind, which everyone hated, powering a wagon? Rufe had called it a wind wagon.

The sheriff ignored noise from the cell room. Whatever was required he had to see this contraption.

He would and sooner than he thought.

The news carried like wildfire. Mostly, jokes were concocted; some were elaborate and some were downright scornful.

By mid-afternoon with the wind down to an occasional gust and the sheriff and Rufe in the jailhouse, two men entered, one tall, one shorter.

Both wore soiled barn coats and baggy, unclean trousers. Sheriff Corning recognized them instantly and half rose from his chair.

Jake Holzer did the talking. He said, 'You heard. It's all around town an' most likely beyond.

'I couldn't tell you last night, Sheriff. I come as close as I could when I said there wasn't a horse alive that could catch it.'

Rufe said, 'Where's Lefler?'

'In a shed across the alley tied like a turkey. We knew what the settlers figured to do last night an' I personally thought it would only get the whole town fired up against us. I figured, too, that without Lefler the settlers wouldn't have no reason to stay in town. One thing, Sheriff, my wind boat stampeded the horses on a north-bound stage.'

Corning knew this. He said, 'Who built the thing, Mister Holzer?'

'I did. I been on my claim three years. There had to be a reason for wind. I tried the idea on a wheel barrow. I went to work in a shed. The sail had to be big enough. I experimented. Twice I drove the rig after dark when no one'd be around. I had to make a bigger sail.'

Horace returned from the eatery, eyed the settler and nodded as he went to the same bench where Rufe was sitting.

The sheriff said, 'You boys go fetch Lefler,' and after they'd gone the sheriff leaned on his desk eyeing the settler. 'The feller from the stage company was here earlier. He said your contraption scairt the stage team so bad they tried to stampede an' overturned the coach. Mister Holzer, you don't suppose you could peddle your wind wagon to the stage company?'

'It only works when the wind's blowing, Sheriff.'

Corning nodded dryly about that. In the Laramie Plains country the wind always blew.

Jonas Lefler appeared from out back with a deputy on each side, he looked at Jake Holzer then at the sheriff as he said, 'Liked to scairt the whey out of me, Al. I never moved so fast before in my life in their rattlin', groanin', damned bean wagon.'

The sheriff eyed Lefler in silence for a time before speaking. 'They saved your life, Jonas. After they took you away in their contraption, Bertram came in loaded for bear. They wanted your hide.' The sheriff paused before saying, 'Jonas, those two squatters saved your miserable damned life.'

Lefler nodded. He already knew this. 'All the same I don't never want to ride in their wind wagon again. I tell you, Al, that thing went so fast I figured . . . '

'Jonas! They saved you from a hanging.'

The cowman considered Sheriff Corning from squinty eyes. 'I know that an' you already said it.'

'Jonas, you old bastard, you owe 'em.'

This time the cowman's eyes narrowed

nearly closed but he said nothing.

'Jonas, *you owe 'em!*'

Lefler licked his lips. 'Is that all you got to say. How many times . . .'

'Listen to me, Jonas, in front of these other gents, you know what your life's worth? To me, a lead cartwheel; to you, a heap more.'

'You should've been a preacher, Sheriff!'

'Ten beeves a year, Jonas, drove over to them. Or as far as I'm concerned they can have you.'

Lefler sat down. With all eyes in the room on him he leaned with both hands between his knees staring at the floor.

Someone none of them had heard hit the door, made it bounce off the wall and stopped dead still at sight of Lefler. The sheriff said, 'Mister Bertram . . .'

'Shut up, Sheriff. Stand up you old bastard.'

Lefler straightened up but did not arise.

Rufe drew his sidearm without haste and cocked it. 'Bertram, just listen. Sit down an' listen. *Sit down!*'

Bertram sat but glared. He seemed about to speak when Al Corning spoke first. 'Mister Bertram, Jonas Lefler'll drive ten steers over to the settlers every year.'

'After what he's done he owes . . . '

Rufe tipped up the gun barrel. 'Just listen,' he said. Bertram threw a menacing look at Rufe Kelly but remained silent.

Sheriff Corning spoke again without looking at Lefler. 'Mister Lefler'll send men over to rebuild what he burnt out an' . . . '

Jonas choked and had a coughing fit. Horace thumped him on the back.

'An' when him'n the other stockmen hire for gathers, markin' time, for whatever gents like Jonas Lefler's need hired hands for, the settlers will have first choice.'

Lefler, red in the face spoke finally, his voice pitched higher than usual. 'I can't say what the other stockmen'll do.'

Corning nodded about that. 'But you can talk to 'em, Jonas. After all, hirin' local men'd be better than waitin' for seasonal riders to come along, which some of 'em never do.'

'Sheriff, I can't . . .'

'Jonas, you know as well as I do an' every man in this room, by rights they'd ought to hang you. This is an olive leaf. You turn it down an' believe me if I can see the smoke from town I'll go up to the Palace and drink to your memory.'

'Ten beeves for Chris' sake, a year?'

Bertram shook his head. 'Fifteen.'

Jonas yanked straight up on his bench. He was red in the face. Sheriff Corning pointed a stiff finger in his direction. Not a word was said.

Lefler stood up. 'Turn my riders loose.'

'Fifteen head, Jonas, drove over to the squatters.'

'Yes. Turn my riders loose, Sheriff.'

Corning smiled. 'Jonas, pay 'em off. Tell 'em if I see a one of 'em in Laramie after tomorrow I'll help the squatters rawhide 'em.'

Lefler's weathered and wrinkled face contorted. 'I got a big outfit to run.'

Sheriff Corning arose nodding. 'Hire your neighbours, Jonas. You got to live with 'em. Maybe in time you'n them'll even get so's you can stand each other . . . Jonas!'

The cowman wanted to speak, he looked from Jake Holzer to Bertram. They looked back. Lefler arose. 'Al Corning . . . '

'I'm right fond of you too, Jonas. I figured you bein' big enough to own a lot of land, herds of cattle, buildings here in town . . . I figured you'd see the light.'

Lefler got as far as the door before facing the sheriff to say, 'Al, I owe you, you connivin', coyote, danged screwt.'

Horace went out with Lefler. As they walked in the direction of the livery barn Horace said, 'Tell about that wind wagon.'

Lefler's squinty eyes sprang wide. 'It went faster'n a steam train. I knew I was goin' to get killed. It went so blamed fast water from my eyes went out the sides.'

'Mister Lefler, would you figure there might be a market from such a contraption?'

The cowman stopped stone still. 'Are you crazy, Deputy? That danged thing? You couldn't run it on the roads, it scares horses so bad they go crazy. Deputy, you want to live good an' make money? Buy a saloon.'

THE END

RIDERS OF RIFLE RANGE
Wade Hamilton

Veterinarian Jeff Jones did not like open warfare — but it was there on Scrub Pine grass. When he diagnosed a sick bull on the Endicott ranch as having the contagious blackleg disease, he got involved in the warfare — whether he liked it or not!

BEAR PAW
Nevada Carter

Austin Dailey traded two cows to a pair of Indians for a bay horse, which subsequently disappeared. Tracks led to a secret hideout of fugitive Indians — and cattle thieves. Indians and stockmen co-operated against the rustlers. But it was Pale Woman who acted as interpreter between her people and the rangemen.

THE WEST WITCH
Lance Howard

Detective Quinton Hilcrest journeys west, seeking the Black Hood Bandits' lost fortune. Within hours of arriving in Hags Bend, he is fighting for his life, ensnared with a beautiful outcast the town claims is a witch! Can he save the young woman from the angry mob?

GUNS OF THE PONY EXPRESS
T. M. Dolan

Rich Zennor joined the Pony Express venture at the start, as second-in-command to tough Denning Hartman. But Zennor had the problems of Hartman believing that they had crossed trails in the past, and the fact that he was strongly attached to Hartman's Indian girl, Conchita.

BLACK JO OF THE PECOS
Jeff Blaine

Nobody knew where Black Josephine Callard came from or whither she returned. Deputy U.S. Marshal Frank Haggard would have to exercise all his cunning and ability to stay alive before he could defeat her highly successful gang and solve the mystery.

RIDE FOR YOUR LIFE
Johnny Mack Bride

They rode west, hoping for a new start. Then they met another broken-down casualty of war, and he had a plan that might deliver them from despair. But the only men who would attempt it would be the truly brave — or the desperate. They were both.

THE NIGHTHAWK
Charles Burnham

While John Baxter sat looking at the ruin that arsonists had made of his log house, a stranger rode into the yard. Baxter and Walt Showalter partnered up and re-built the house. But when it was dynamited, they struck back — and all hell broke loose.

MAVERICK PREACHER
M. Duggan

Clay Purnell was hopeful that his posting to Capra would be peaceable enough. However, on his very first day in town he rode into trouble. Although loath to use his .45, Clay found he had little choice — and his likeness to a notorious bank robber didn't help either!

SIXGUN SHOWDOWN
Art Flynn

After years as a lawman elsewhere, Dan Herrick returned to his old Arizona stamping ground to find that nesters were being driven from their homesteads by ruthless ranchers. Before putting away his gun once and for all, Dan forced a bloody and decisive showdown.

RIDE LIKE THE DEVIL!
Sam Gort

Ben Trunch arrived back on the Big T only to find that land-grabbing was in progress. He confronted Luke Fletcher, saloon-keeper and town boss, with what was happening, and was immediately forced to ride for his life. But he got the chance to put it all right in the end.

SLOW WOLF AND DAN FOX:
Larry & Stretch
Marshall Grover

The deck was stacked against an innocent man. Larry Valentine played detective, and his investigation propelled the Texas Trouble-Shooters into a gun-blazing fight to the finish.

BRANAGAN'S LAW
Alan Irwin

To Angus Flint, the valley was his domain and he didn't want any new settlers. But Texas Ranger Jim Branagan had other ideas. Could he put an end to Flint's tyranny for good?

THE DEVIL RODE A PINTO
Bret Rey

When a settler is cut to ribbons in a frenzied attack, Texas Ranger Sam Buck learns that the killer is Rufus Berry, known as The Devil. Sam stiffens his resolve to kill or capture Berry and break up his gang.